Midlothian *our* library

The Scavengers

THE SCAVENGERS

Bill Knox

Constable • London

Constable & Robinson Ltd
3 The Lanchesters
162 Fulham Palace Road
London W6 9ER
www.constablerobinson.com

First published in Great Britain 1964
This edition published in Great Britain by Constable,
an imprint of Constable & Robinson Ltd 2007

A copy of the British Library Cataloguing in Publication
Data is available from the British Library.

ISBN 13: 978-1-84529-471-7
ISBN 10: 1-84529-471-8

Printed and bound in the EU

Chapter One

The night was dark, but in a dozen different, intangible ways the sea's surface still told that fish lay below, fish in quantity and not far from the surface. Standing by his tiny wheelhouse, the fishing-boat skipper read the signs with the ease of a lifetime spent off the Scottish west coast and watched the last of his mile-long swath of seine net go slipping out. With luck, he hoped this one shoot would be enough to complete his catch.

Then he looked again, and the hope died as he saw the phantom-like shape of the trawler grow out of the black night, coming steadily and without lights on a course across his stern. He sensed the invisible impact as the trawler's heavy wire-cabled gear crossed his fragile nets of cotton and cord, tearing a rupturing path of damage. Without slowing, the larger craft continued on her way, her silhouette gradually merging again into the cloaking darkness. A moment later, even the faint sound of her engine had faded.

In all, it took two minutes – and turned the skipper's mood from peaceful anticipation into boiling, bitter rage. He flung himself back into his wheelhouse, grabbed the radio microphone, and began a vehement demand for a Fishery Protection cruiser to 'sort out those piratical blanking vandals', still somewhere out in that apparent emptiness of night.

But the demand, he knew, was probably futile. His ripped nets floated off the shallow Ballantrae Bank, where the rich waters of the Firth of Clyde met the cold currents of the North Channel between Scotland and Ireland. Only an hour before, the guarded gossip of the fishing fleet's radio grapevine had placed the nearest fishery cruiser snug in harbour at Campbeltown, thirty miles away on the Mull of Kintyre.

Fishery Protection cruisers? He scowled. Like any other police outfit, they seemed always to be around when you didn't want them, never there when they were needed.

But for once he happened to be wrong. A protection ship was lying at Campbeltown, just as the grapevine said – but her patrol neighbour, H.M. fishery cruiser *Marlin*, was less than eight miles from the seine boat's position. On her bridge, there was already interest in the two small radar blips that represented seine boat and trawler.

Bow wave creaming high and phosphorescent, *Marlin* closed on the trawler twenty minutes after the radio call. Her twenty-one-inch searchlight glared to life, lanced out at the other vessel, then located and held the name *Tecta* and the Norwegian registration letters beneath. The command 'heave to' came in a busy clatter from an Aldis signal lamp on *Marlin*'s bridge.

For a few stubborn moments the trawler kept on course while *Marlin* slackened speed and ran parallel. The fishery cruiser's deck lights blazed to life, picking out the Blue Ensign at her blunt stern, the motor launch swung out on davits and ready to be lowered. With something close to a sigh, the trawler's diesel exhaust note settled to a slow, gentle throb. She lost way and lay rocking gently in the swell, drift-anchored by her nets, her crew watching silently while the patrol ship nosed closer.

A fishery officer looks for few formalities and fewer welcomes when he boards a suspect. Chief Officer Webb Carrick, *Marlin*'s first mate, scrambled aboard the trawler's port quarter from the swaying launch that had brought him alongside, waited a moment while three more of *Marlin*'s crew followed him on to the low searchlight-bathed deck, then strode forward to the small, heavily moustached Norwegian skipper whose ancient peaked cap marked him out from the rest of his crew.

'Again, Mr Carrick?' The Norwegian spoke in carefully

accented English and gave a rueful grimace which sent the longtailed moustache still lower towards his chin. 'There is some trouble, eh?'

Carrick balanced his chunky frame as the trawler's deck rolled, and returned the grimace, a faint twinkle in his eyes. 'There's trouble, Skipper. Trawling within the three-mile limit, fishing without lights, running through set nets –' The catalogue gave him a certain amount of satisfaction. Twice before *Marlin* had caught up with Hendrick Munsen and his *Tecta*, twice before the Norwegian had managed to wriggle out from under the charges of illegal fishing hanging over him.

'The limit?' Munsen shoved his cap further back and scratched the close-cropped grey hair beneath. 'But we are outside the limit, Mr Carrick! To trawl within it – no, we would not do that.' He turned, gazed mournfully past his silent, watchful crew, and gave a hail.

'Mamma!'

A large shape moved inside the *Tecta*'s wheelhouse, a door banged open, and Helga Munsen emerged. The other half of the Munsen partnership, large and shapeless beneath a voluminous oilskin coat, gave Carrick a beaming, broken-toothed smile which seemed to split her leathery face.

'Position, Hendrick?' The voice was one no Atlantic storm could have smothered.

Her spouse nodded.

'Six miles west of Bennane Head,' declared Helga Munsen triumphantly. 'I 'ave checked, Hendrick.'

'It is now.' Carrick spoke with acquired patience. 'What was it half an hour ago?'

'Perhaps the same. And we have lights.' Hendrick Munsen thumbed blandly towards the red, white and green triangle of fishing lights on the trawler's foremast.

'I know. I saw them switch on as we came over,' agreed Carrick mildly. 'Haul in the trawl, please, Skipper.'

The *Tecta*'s crew stirred to life, clustering that little bit nearer, and Carrick sensed as much as saw his boarding party ease into flanking positions beside him. If there was to be trouble, it would come now.

'The trawl, please, Skipper.'

Hendrick Munsen chewed one tail of his moustache and glanced at his wife. She shrugged. Munsen chewed harder, looked down at the toes of his heavy seaboots, across towards the brightly lit *Marlin*, then gave an upward wave of his hand.

The Norwegians set to work, a team of craftsmen in heavy sweaters, and torn overalls, working with a casual, swift efficiency. First *Tecta*'s winch engine spluttered to life, then, as her capstan drum began to turn and overhead lamps blazed on throughout the fish-deck area, the wire ropes of the giant trawl stirred and the wind-in commenced.

'Bo'sun.' Carrick winked at the nearest of his tiny boarding party. 'Tell *Marlin* they're co-operating.'

'Aye, aye, sir.' Petty Officer William 'Clapper' Bell, six feet of bulkily muscular Glasgow-Irishman, said it almost regretfully as he unhitched his signal torch and turned towards the trawler rail. Better luck next time perhaps – he began thumbing the torch button.

Many turns of wet, glistening cable were round the winch drum before the giant trawl net's mouth broke surface. Side by side, Carrick and the *Tecta*'s skipper walked forward as the otter boards – the big wooden 'wings' that held the bag of the net open under water – came over the vessel's side.

'Rub marks on both boards – the sort of mark you'd get from a rope.' Carrick was politely observant.

'Been there since long time back,' said the Norwegian uneasily.

Behind them, the winch engine changed its note and *Tecta*'s foremast pulleys creaked as the main bag of the net came up on its sling. A vast, water-drenching mass bulged by a struggling, wriggling multitude of speckled silver shapes, the trawl swung inboard, swaying to a halt over the foredeck. A trawlerman jerked the release cord at the

8

net's end core and a gasping, flapping harvest of fish cascaded across the deck plates.

'Like to explain that, Skipper?' Carrick pointed upwards, to where the overhead lights showed a torn, tattered remnant of seine net hanging tangled in the trawl's thicker mesh.

Munsen gave a soft curse of dismay. But the Norwegian was ignoring the evidence above him, staring instead towards the hillocking fish.

Two of his men were already there, pushing the dripping folds of net aside, shovelling a bare-handed path through their catch towards the larger, darker shape which lay in its midst. Wading ankle-deep in the slippery, living carpet, Carrick was across and by their side as they cleared a partial space around.

Clad from head to foot in a black rubber cold-weather suit, lying draped in a debris of fish scales and bottom weed, the frogman had been dead for some time. The twin compressed-air cylinders of his aqualung unit were still on his back, but the mouthpiece of the breathing tube hung free. His glass-fronted face mask had protected the upper part of his features, but chin and cheeks showed the attentions of dogfish and other nibbling life. Carrick gauged him to have been middle-aged, and could guess his identity. Marine biologists of the Fishery Research branch were closely enough allied to the Protection Service to make their going missing a priority concern, and Dr Ernest Elgin's disappearance ten days previously had caused considerable turmoil.

'What we do now, eh?' Skipper Munsen cocked his head in birdlike style towards Carrick, hopeful that this larger discovery might avoid the awkwardness of his own situation.

Carrick made a cursory inspection of the dead biologist's scuba gear before he answered. It was a standard type, close enough to the equipment he often used himself, and even the rubber suit appeared intact.

'First I use your loud-hailer to talk to *Marlin*,' he

decided. 'After that, Skipper, my guess is we head for harbour.'

The megaphoned exchange between Carrick and the watchful, waiting fishery cruiser took little time. Captain Shannon, *Marlin*'s commander, was never fond of wasting words and his decision was a carbon copy of his second-in-command's intention.

'Head for Ayr, Mr Carrick,' his voice boomed across the gap of water. 'I'll radio in, and have a reception committee waiting.' Then, an afterthought. 'Better keep an eye on his trawl. Somebody might just try to get rid of that piece of seine net.'

Carrick waved an acknowledgement, and calculated. It was three a.m. That meant they'd reach the port of Ayr about dawn, just before high water. Already *Marlin*'s twin-screw wake was beginning to gather, and the fishery cruiser was moving away. Herring were back in the Firth, vast schools of the blue-backed fish in numbers greater than for many a long year, following the irresistible pull of their plankton food; and where the herring tide went, the fishing fleets of half a dozen nations followed, intent on filling their nets. There were an estimated four hundred boats of all types and conditions at work in the Firth, squabbling, quarrelling, sometimes coming close to sinking under the sheer weight of their catches, and *Marlin* had plenty of work awaiting.

'We'll steer north-nor'-east,' Carrick told the glum Norwegian as the fishery cruiser curved away into the darkness. 'Your fishing trip's over for a spell.'

Munsen nodded. 'Okay, I tell Mamma. Then, what the hell, we have breakfast. You like fish?' He interpreted Carrick's wry expression, and made diplomatic amends. 'Well, maybe we got some bacon. I ask Mamma – she'll see.'

A grey, rain-promising dawn was climbing over the Ayrshire hills towards the steel-blue, wave-tufted sea, as the

10

trawler came below the high Dunure cliffs, then moved into the bay beyond.

Dark exhaust smoke puttering from their slender stacks, a small armada of wooden-hulled seine and ring netters were coming out of Ayr Harbour with the tide, flanked by a scattering of tiny line-boats. One group veered towards the incoming trawler, their bright paintwork and gleaming varnish in sharp contrast to the scowling faces that glared towards the *Tecta*'s comparative bulk.

Fists shook from the nearest of the in-shore boats – then a roar of delight went up as the men aboard saw the blue-uniformed Fishery Patrol party grouped round the trawler's wheelhouse.

'Always somebody feels happy, eh?' Skipper Munsen leaned gloomily against the *Tecta*'s steering wheel as, one after another, his tormentors sailed in closer to jeer and wave. 'You know what happens to us three nights back? We are in the North Channel, and somebody starts shooting at us with a rifle. Keep off – well, we don't argue.'

'Recognize the other boat?' Carrick sipped a fresh mug of tea, not particularly surprised. There had been more than one outbreak of rifle and shotgun clashes since the herring had crowded in, but so far the shots had been high and wide, temperamental threats rather than deliberate deeds.

'Perhaps.' Mamma Munsen answered for her husband. It was second nature for the big Norwegian woman, whose duties ranged from helping Hendrick Munsen run the *Tecta* to acting as cook for their crew of ten. 'But what difference? Our people have come here since the Viking long-ships raided, Mr Carrick. We don't run away – not far, anyway.' She inspected Carrick with unconcealed interest. Helga Munsen was long past youth, but that didn't mean she had lost a sense of academic appreciation.

Perhaps it was the naval uniform, the thick-soled sea-boots, and white, roll-necked sweater – Helga had always liked a seaman, which was why she'd married her Hendrick in the first instance, when he was a second engineer on a Bergen whaler. This fishery officer wasn't perfect of course, but few men were. Five ten in height, stockily built, dark-brown eyes and darker brown hair – perhaps he was thirty, perhaps less, it was hard to tell with those broad-boned, weather-bronzed features. He seemed even younger when he smiled, yet he was a little too thin in the lips to support the theory that this was a man of easy-going outlook. A difficult man to rule, she decided. Not like Hendrick. Yes, there were compensations in having a husband like Hendrick. . .

'How long you think you hold us once we get in?' she asked hopefully. Every hour lost from the fishing grounds represented fewer, good, hard Norwegian kroners being built up in their bank account back at Bergen.

'Depends on a lot of things.' Carrick watched a tiny smack – coiled, ready-baited lines crowding most of its stern – weave a perilous path across their bow. 'A day, maybe two. Once *Marlin* comes in, it shouldn't take long.'

For two years now, Webb Carrick had been in the Fishery Protection Service, and he still found it difficult to think of himself as both sea-going policeman and civil servant. Yet that was exactly what the job amounted to – that, and perhaps a little more. The patrol officers and men might wear naval uniform, their warship-grey fishery cruisers, just a little bigger than the largest trawlers, might have the outward appearance of fast naval gunboats and possessed at least an equal turn of speed. But their task as government employees was to police the fishing grounds, to act as both watchdogs and nursemaids over the fishing fleets, to keep law and order along the vast stretches of coastal waters and beyond which constituted the work area of an industry with a multimillion-pound annual turnover.

In Carrick's case, the transition had been near to accidental. A newly gained, deep-sea master's ticket in his pocket, he'd had the choice of sailing as second mate on a freighter on the Liverpool–Boston 'bus run' route or taking a slightly shaky first mate's berth on a rust-bucket tramp bound for the Far East. Instead, he'd suddenly found himself being interviewed on the strength of a long-forgotten application, and had finished the day with the appointment as chief officer on *Marlin*, signing the black-covered warrant card that gave Webster Carrick the powers and pay of an assistant superintendent of fisheries.

Marlin, like the rest of her flotilla, covered an average of 17,000 sea miles a year, patrolling her beat from the Butt of Lewis in the north down to the southern limits of the Solway. No guns were mounted on her 180-foot length, with its distinctive high-raked bow and squat, single funnel. She ruled by the thirty-knot speed of her 2000-h.p., twin-screw engines, by the authority of her Blue Ensign with its gold-crowned laurel-wreath badge, and by the gruff, decisive character of Captain Shannon, her commander. Shannon rated as a superintendent of fisheries – that gave him the power to act as his own judge and jury in a wide range of offences.

Fishermen would say that it was almost impossible to make a living without every so often breaking or bending the rules. Maybe they were right. But the basics were constant – line and small-net boats could work inside the three-mile limit, so could lobster boats and the like. Bigger net boats and the trawlers had to stay outside. There were plenty of complications – local rules, like the one which barred British trawlers absolutely from working in the whole area of the Firth of Clyde, protecting it as a breeding ground.

That was one rule which couldn't be imposed on non-British registered trawlers like the *Tecta*, which could fish where they chose provided they stayed outside territorial waters. They could fish all right – but an offender would find himself banned from landing his catch. Not that that worried these visitors. They filled their refrigerated fish holds, then headed at full speed for the Continental markets.

Carrick shook his head. Two years, and the Fishery Laws still had their complex mazes when he tried to make sense of it all. But at least some of the boat skippers had a simpler code – follow the fish, inshore or far out, fill the holds, get the market. Munsen had done it. Well, it would be up to Shannon to decide what happened next to the Norwegian, and Carrick had learned not to attempt to forecast his captain's reactions.

Ayr Harbour was comparatively empty when the *Tecta* nosed her way into dock, obeying berthing instructions which sent her over to the south quay, where two black saloon cars and a mortuary hearse were waiting. Nearer the harbour mouth, a couple of coasters loaded coal close to a large nitrate boat that rode high and empty. Further up, a handful of late-arrival seine netters were sending up box after box of fish to the quayside, where the usual gathering of trade buyers were already bidding.

Across the harbour, a solitary trawler was tied to the north quay, a string of washing fluttering around her stern. Carrick had seen her before – the *Karmona* had come up from the Milford Haven area two months before, was Irish-registered, and, in keeping with her antiquated lines, seemed to spend most of her time in port, broken down, her engine being stripped for yet another repair.

The *Tecta*'s bow and stern ropes were barely secured and her narrow gangway down before the first of her visitors emerged from the two waiting cars and came bustling aboard. Carrick was there to meet him, Petty Officer Clapper Bell in attendance a few paces to the rear – when a Chief Superintendent of Fisheries came a-calling, it paid a bo'sun to be organized.

'Morning, sir.' Carrick performed the nearest he could achieve to a regulation salute, conscious of Clapper Bell rigid at attention in the background, of the interested audience viewing the proceedings from the trawler wheelhouse.

'Morning.' Commander Dobie, in dark lounge suit, high-polished shoes, and stiff white collar, was a small man. He also happened to have commanded a Far East m.t.b. flotilla in World War Two, where he had earned a double D.S.O.; but the days were gone when he could regard being on

14

a quayside at dawn with anything but disgust. 'Well, Carrick, where's the body?'

'Aft, sir. In one of the storerooms. Do you want to . . .'

'See it? Hell, no. Not yet, anyway. I'm not a pathologist, Mr Carrick – haven't eaten, either.' Commander Dobie gave a quick, gnomish grin. 'Still thriving, bo'sun? And ugly as ever, eh?'

'Sir!' Clapper Bell beamed with delight at the recognition. He'd earned one of the medal ribbons on his P.O.'s monkey jacket on the same m.t.b. flotilla, during a turbulent day off the Rangoon coast.

Commander Dobie remembered the rest of the group of visitors waiting patiently behind him on the gangway. 'Felt I'd better come along in the circumstances. This is Chief Inspector Deacon, county police, Professor MacEwan from the Fishery Research Department, and Dr Lonson – Lonson is medical, MacEwan is here to establish identification.'

Professor MacEwan, thin, stringy beneath a heavy tweed coat, his sparse white hair ruffled by the slight breeze, was the last to shake hands.

'Best get this over with, I suppose. Chief Inspector, once it's done I presume we can – ah – move him ashore?'

The policeman nodded. 'I'll come with you if you don't mind, sir. Just for the report.'

Carrick nodded to Clapper Bell. 'Bo'sun, show them the way, will you?'

Petty Officer Bell shepherded the biologist and policeman aft, Dr Lonson trailing behind. When Carrick turned again, he found Commander Dobie eyeing the *Tecta*'s trawl, where the telltale strip of seine net remained as it had been found.

'Seems clear cut enough,' ruminated the Chief Superintendent of Fisheries. 'Inside the limit when he began trawling, wasn't he?' He took out a thin much-battered silver cigarette case. 'Smoke?'

'Thank you, sir.' Carrick accepted a light from a matching silver lighter. 'His story is he was just outside, but Captain Shannon has gone back to check on the seine netter's position.'

'The *Tecta* – that's our crafty Norwegian friend Munsen.' Dobie permitted himself a thin chuckle. 'Time we nailed him. Still, I'll leave that to Shannon. How long d'you reckon she was trawling before you boarded her?'

'Not much more than the half-hour, sir. I'd say they were about ready to haul in anyway when we arrived.' Carrick was slightly puzzled.

'Makes it difficult to say exactly where they collected our biologist, eh?' Commander Dobie took a short, quick puff at his cigarette. 'Well, ten days in the water, negative buoyancy, tide and currents – position's about right. Dr Elgin went missing off Culzean Bay. Flip-flapping around on his own, gathering sea snails and similar – you know what the Fishery Research outfit's like.' The Chief Superintendent left his own opinion in little doubt. 'You checked his gear, I suppose?'

Carrick nodded. 'Seemed all right, sir.'

'That's surprising, isn't it?' Commander Dobie gave a sniff of interest. 'Well, isn't it?'

'Depends on a lot of things.' Carrick tossed his cigarette over the trawler's side, heard the soft sizzle as it met the water. 'Depends on the depth he was working, how he was working, things like that. Diving has occupational hazards – just like any other job of work. The trouble is, in diving they creep up on you without much warning.'

'I'll take your word for it – I'm no expert.' Commander Dobie shrugged, then gave a faint scowl. 'I'll make sure his outfit is kept intact until the post-mortem report gives us a better picture. Then, if it was illness, that's an end to it. But if something went wrong, any number of departmental desk polishers are going to want to know why and how.'

'Any idea why he was in the bay alone, sir?' It was the one point that didn't quite make sense to Carrick. There was nothing unusual about Fishery Research staff skin-diving in the course of their work, but it was routine for them to operate from a manned boat.

'Some kind of last-minute hitch in arrangements.' Dobie glanced impatiently at his watch. 'Elgin was making some off-shore surveys, routine stuff, pure routine, but it seems he decided to put in some unofficial overtime. His daughter was to have been with him, and then she couldn't make it.'

He brightened as the rest of his party re-emerged, their task completed. 'Anyway, I'll want you up at the mortuary later, to inspect the gear again. Bring along a written report about finding the body, will you? Keeps the paperwork under control, and Lord knows, there's enough of that already.'

Professor MacEwan, in the lead, was sombre-faced when he rejoined them a moment later. 'It's Dr Elgin,' confirmed the Fishery Research man. 'No doubt about it. But he's – what I mean is, I suppose you'll need a second identification, for corroboration?'

'Ask the police about that,' said Dobie. 'That's their side of the business.'

'Thinking of his daughter?' Chief Inspector Deacon pursed his lips. 'I think we can avoid that, the way things are. Another colleague would be enough, as far as I'm concerned.'

MacEwan was relieved. 'And the post mortem?'

'I can get through it this morning, once I've had breakfast,' the police surgeon chipped in from the rear. 'You'll have my report by eleven.'

Carrick watched them leave, and a moment later the mortuary hearse began to purr closer to the *Tecta*. He turned away, heading back to the trawler's wheelhouse. If Hendrick Munsen felt his own little part in the situation might be forgotten, he was in for a disappointment.

Prompt on eleven a.m., Webb Carrick arrived at the County Hospital mortuary annex. Clapper Bell drove him over from the harbour, using the Fishery Department's dark-blue Humber station wagon, and it was due to Petty Officer Bell's almost unnatural ability to beg, borrow, and otherwise acquire that Carrick stepped out clean-shaven, uniform pressed, wearing shoes only a shade too tight for comfort, and with a fresh white shirt. *Marlin*'s boarding parties didn't include overnight bags among their equipment.

'Want me to wait, sir?' The burly petty officer raised a cautious, questioning eyebrow.

'No, I'll make my own way back.' Carrick grinned at the big Glasgow-Irishman. 'Supposing you take a wander around the harhour area and get a sniff of what's going on among the fishing crews. But, Clapper –'

'Sir?' Clapper Bell put just the right amount of innocent inquiry into his voice.

'Keep out of trouble. Stick to beer – right?'

'Right, sir.' Bell gave a solemn nod and once Carrick slammed the station-wagon door, the Humber set off in a wheel-spun cloud of gravel dust.

Inside the hospital annex, a white-coated attendant directed him to a small, cream-washed office at the end of a short, disinfectant-aired corridor.

There were three people in the room. Professor Mac-Ewan, the Fishery Research chief, stood over by the window and turned expectantly as Carrick entered. Lonson, the police surgeon, was behind the only desk, and to one side sat a girl in her early twenties. She was slim, petite, and dressed in a grey corduroy two piece. Cut in a short fringe, her brunette hair held a hint of copper among its locks and framed a snub-nosed face which was pale beneath an outdoor tan.

MacEwan handled the introductions. 'Helen, this is Chief Officer Carrick, the Fishery Protection officer I told you about. Carrick, this is Dr Elgin's daughter.'

She looked at him in silence for a moment, her hazel eyes showing the tired heaviness of recent strain. When she spoke, it was with a forced steadiness. 'You found my father, Mr Carrick. Dr MacEwan says you checked his scuba equipment.'

'Only roughly,' Carrick told her. 'Conditions weren't ideal at the time. But I'm going to give it a fuller inspection – that's partly why I'm here.'

'You're qualified to do it?' Helen Elgin ignored the gathering frown on MacEwan's lined, elderly face. 'Plenty of

18

people go free-diving, Mr Carrick, I've done it. But that doesn't make me – or them experts.'

'I'm qualified,' Carrick assured her. A two-month posting to a Royal Navy course in self-contained underwater-breathing apparatus, to give scuba gear its Sunday name, didn't leave many gaps. A team of instructors who believed in making you learn lessons the hard way, via their deep-diving tanks, made sure of that.

'Something went wrong, I'm sure of it.' The girl bit her lip. 'I want to find out, Mr Carrick. I'm determined to find out.'

MacEwan crossed over and laid a thin, bony hand on her shoulder. 'If there was –' he heavily accented the word – 'then we'll find it, Helen.' For Carrick's benefit, he explained. 'Helen was called on to work late that evening, at the last minute. Now she has the idea in her head that if her father hadn't been alone in the boat, if she'd been with him, this wouldn't have happened. I told her she needn't come here today.' He shrugged at the uselessness of it. 'But she insisted.'

Helen Elgin looked up at her father's colleague. 'You've heard the post-mortem findings, Professor MacEwan. Don't they say I'm right? Or would you rather have Mr Carrick's opinion?' Her hands formed small, tight fists on her lap.

'It was an accident, and you couldn't have prevented it.' Dr Lonson spoke up. The police surgeon's manner was both anxious and earnest. 'Miss Elgin, you've got to understand that.'

'What was the result, Doctor?' Carrick felt a growing urge to help the dark-haired girl find some relief from her tension.

Lonson tapped the scribbled pencil notes on the desk before him. 'I'm just drafting the report now. Dr Elgin's body had been in the water approximately ten days – since he disappeared, as one might expect. Death was due to anoxia, causing cardiac failure.'

'Anoxia?'

'In this case, it could be called oxygen starvation.' The

police surgeon glanced significantly towards the girl. 'The exact details aren't necessary, but it comes to this. Dr Elgin didn't drown. The condition of the lungs and other organs makes that clear. But the blood haemoglobin count shows an excessive presence of carbon dioxide. I'd hazard that for some reason he wasn't getting a sufficient air supply from his apparatus, that he didn't realize the fact until probably too late, that he then lapsed into coma, followed almost immediately by failure of the respiratory centre. The mouthpiece would fall free, of course, and there was a slight intake of sea water thereafter.' He cleared his throat apologetically. 'It's difficult to put it into simpler terms.'

'Maybe I can,' said Carrick softly. 'We call it "beating the lung". It happens if you're working hard, too hard, under water. That way you're – well, trying to use more air than you're taking from the cylinder. I've seen a man go into a blackout as a result.'

'But there was somebody there to help your man,' said Helen Elgin, her voice ragged. 'Wasn't there?'

Carrick had to agree. 'There was. But there was an element of luck in it too. Another time, even with someone beside him, he might have died. Look it up in the text-books if you don't believe me.'

'I'll believe you.' She seemed to gain some comfort from his words. 'Mr Carrick, you're going to check the diving gear now?'

'Yes.'

'Will you let me be there, to watch you?'

Carrick hesitated, but Dr Lonson gave a slow grunt of approval. 'I think that might be a good idea, Carrick. Unorthodox, but good.'

'All right, then.' Carrick had no objection. 'Professor MacEwan, as Elgin's immediate chief, you'll know what work he was engaged on when he vanished?'

The elderly marine biologist rubbed his chin with one hand. 'Aye, most of it. What do you want to know?'

'What depth was he probably working at in Culzean Bay, what specifically was he doing, and how long might he have expected to be down?'

'That's fairly simple to answer,' said MacEwan. 'Elgin was working from his own boat, a small launch. It was bow-anchored about two hundred yards off shore. Elgin went out the previous evening, at low tide, so that he'd be working near the ten-fathoms mark. Yes, about sixty feet.'

'Any spare air bottles in the boat?'

'No.' It was Helen Elgin who answered. 'Dad said it wouldn't take him very long to do what he wanted – that he'd only be down a matter of minutes. He'd already collected most of the specimens he needed.'

'What kind of specimens? Weed, bottom life, or fish?'

'Weed and bottom life.' MacEwan elected to answer. 'Part of a regular sampling programme from the bay Elgin has –' he corrected himself awkwardly – 'had been engaged on for the past eight or nine months. He'd gone under in that area any number of times before.'

'Thanks.' It gave Carrick at least a basic picture of the situation. 'When Commander Dobie comes, will you tell him where I am?'

Dr Lonson nodded. 'The attendant on duty will show you where we've put the diving kit. It hasn't been handled more than was necessary.'

Dr Elgin's diving gear was lying on a bench in an otherwise empty workshop shed attached to the hospital garage. The attendant opened the door, switched on the overhead lights, then left Carrick and the girl alone. As the door closed, she walked forward to the bench and looked down at the rubber suit, by now a dry, shapeless bundle.

'If it happened as they said, it wouldn't have taken long, would it?'

'As far as he was concerned, no. It would creep up on him. He just wouldn't be aware of it until almost the end.'

'Thank you.' She pursed her lips. 'He was never very fond of this, you know. In fact, at first he almost hated having to go down. He didn't have to, of course – his real job was in the laboratory. But he could collect his own

21

specimens this way, without relying on others, and that was important to him.'

'I've met men like that.' Carrick took out his cigarettes, gave her one, helped himself, then lit both. 'They're inclined to be stubborn, but usually pretty likeable. What about the rest of the family?'

She shook her head. 'None, apart from a couple of distant cousins somewhere. My mother died two years ago – this is the first time I've felt almost glad about it. This would have broken her.' She took another quick puff at her cigarette. 'Well, where will you start?'

'The suit first.' Carrick lifted it from the bench. Dr Elgin had been using a neoprene foam-rubber 'wet' suit, the type which, while it didn't keep a diver dry, trapped an initial layer of water between rubber and the diver's body and thus built up its own warmth. He inspected its surface inch by inch, brushing aside the odd specklings of weed and fish scales left from the *Tecta*'s trawl. Here and there were occasional areas where the rubber had been grazed by undersea contacts. A cycle-tube patch on one elbow showed where an old tear had been repaired.

'I fixed that for him.' The girl gave a taut smile of remembrance. 'He was exploring a wreck off shore, looking for sea snails, when a conger popped out and chased him off.'

Six or seven feet of angry needle-mouthed conger eel made a pretty potent reason for leaving any area. Carrick set down the suit, feeling a gradual, growing awareness of the type of man Dr Elgin had been.

'Suit's all right. Small stuff next.' The wrist depth gauge was intact, but was a constant-reading type, and told nothing. Only one flipper had been recovered, the other could have been lost anywhere. Carrick frowned over the next item, the doctor's weight belt. The row of separate lead weights, used to counteract the positive buoyancy of air cylinders and suit, were completely intact. He tried fastening, then unsnapping the belt's quick-release buckle, and found it worked smoothly.

'Something wrong?' Helen Elgin was watching him closely.

He shook his head. 'Just wondering about a possibility. Let's check the aqualung.'

The dead biologist's equipment, though not the most modern, seemed both adequate and well maintained. It was a standard twin set, the harness frame carrying two 1200-litre air bottles with joining manifold. Shut-off valve, regulator, breathing tube – Carrick examined each with minute care. The valve was wide open, the demand regulator's needle valve slid smooth and trouble free, its non-return valve for freeing exhaled air was in perfect order.

'Well?' She stood back, anxiously expectant.

'Nothing, Helen. Absolutely nothing. Your father's equipment was perfect. I'd use it myself this minute, without a worry.'

She accepted it quietly, but with a trace of bewilderment. 'Then it was just that – that he – what did you call it?'

'Beat the lung,' Carrick told her. 'Put out too much energy.' As a final check, he disconnected the breath tube and blew through the mouthpiece. The tube was free of blockages. 'There's a rock shelf over quite a part of the bay. Plenty of broken boulders, weed, other things. Maybe he became trapped, and was trying to free himself, maybe it was just plain overwork.' Fingers moving almost automatically, he reconnected the breath tube while he spoke. 'This sampling programme he was working on – did your father ever talk about running into trouble on other dives?'

Helen Elgin shook her head. 'He did it once a week, every week – ever since Crosslodge opened and the programme began.'

'Crosslodge?' The name was a surprise. Crosslodge nuclear station, latest in the chain of uranium-fuelled power stations feeding the British electricity grid, was situated on the north side of Culzean Bay. It looked across to Culzean Castle, the National Trust showpiece sometimes described as Eisenhower Towers. The castle's top floor, gifted to the General as a permanent Scottish home after the Normandy invasion, now didn't have quite the view it enjoyed before Crosslodge reared up on the opposite skyline, but so far nobody had complained. 'What's the link between marine biology and the nuclear boffins?'

'Purely incidental,' she told him. 'A safety measure, I suppose you'd call it. Crosslodge uses a lot of water for cooling – takes it straight from the sea, then releases it in again. One of Dad's Fishery Research assignments was to keep an eye on marine samples from the area, from plankton upwards, and make sure they didn't show any unusual signs.'

'Of radiation?'

She smiled completely this time, and the change was as from winter to spring. 'I'm sorry, Mr Carrick –'

'The name's Webb.'

'Webb. I'm sorry, but I know the kind of ideas that the word "nuclear" can give people. But Dad's work was perfectly straightforward, and so is Crosslodge. I should know. I'm a secretary in the plant office – and we've positively no secrets at Crosslodge, and very glad of it too. It saves all sorts of complications.' She took a last glance at the aqualung equipment. 'I – well, I'd like to thank you for letting me see this. Maybe I still blame myself – but I've got a much saner outlook on it now.'

Carrick went with her towards the door, opened it, and followed her out.

'You're going home?'

'Yes.' They were in the open, and there was a slight drizzle of rain in the air. 'I've got friends outside with a car.'

He walked with her round the edge of the hospital block and over towards the car park. Then, with a grunt of regret, he slowed. A black police car had just stopped at the hospital's main door, disgorging Commander Dobie and Chief Inspector Deacon. The two men went straight into the building.

'Time you went back?' The girl's manner was oddly sympathetic. 'This all means quite a lot of extra trouble for you, doesn't it?'

'Trouble's our business, and your father was in Fishery

Research. That makes it family business as far as we're concerned. You'll be all right – at home, I mean?'

She nodded. 'One of the girls from Crosslodge is staying with me at the flat – for the next few days, anyway.' Then she hesitated. 'If – well, if anything else happens, you'll let me know?'

'I'll let you know.' He watched her go, her stiletto heels tapping their way over the concrete. As she reached the parked cars, an engine growled to life and a small red M.G. 1100 saloon pulled forward towards her. It stopped, she got into the front passenger seat, and almost immediately the car was under way again. As it swept past, he had a quick glimpse of the two other occupants – the driver, a tall, dark-haired man with a thin moustache and, leaning forward from the rear seat, a raven-haired girl in a sheepskin jacket, worn open and showing a flash of well-curved yellow sweater beneath. Then the M.G. had gone, heading in towards the town, brake lights winking momentarily as it eased into the main traffic flow.

Carrick stood there a moment before he went back into the hospital. He found Commander Dobie and the policeman already settled in Dr Lonson's office, but there was no sign of MacEwan. The Fishery Research chief had already left.

'Gone back to report to his bosses in Edinburgh,' explained Lonson briefly. 'I've told Commander Dobie and Chief Inspector Deacon the extent of the autopsy findings.'

'They're straightforward enough,' agreed Deacon, settling back in his chair. 'We'll need the usual court hearing later, of course – but thank heaven, a Scottish fatal accident inquiry's a lot more simple and civilized than an English inquest.' He beamed around him. 'All wrapped up, bar the formalities, eh?'

Commander Dobie gave a nod of more cautious agreement. 'Looks that way. What about the diving equipment, Carrick? Find anything unusual about it?'

'Nothing, sir. All in perfect condition. But –' Carrick

phrased it cautiously – 'there are a couple of, well, unusual features.'

'Unusual?' Commander Dobie raised a questioning eyebrow.

'This work he was carrying out for Crosslodge nuclear station, sir. It wouldn't call for particularly heavy exertion. Then the time factor involved, and the air supply left – they're both unknown quantities.'

'I'm well aware of the Crosslodge work, Carrick.' Commander Dobie's manner was cooled. 'Strictly routine – Dr Elgin's connection with Crosslodge is both slight and immaterial. That, in case you're wondering, is the only reason I didn't mention it. And I'm also well aware that divers working on their own can get into a variety of underwater difficulties, difficulties that can mean considerable exertion when they're trying to get free.'

Carrick nodded. 'I know, sir. But, well, I'd like to – to tidy it up a little more. Take a look around his diving position for myself.'

Dr Lonson gave a faint chuckle. 'And come up with an explanation perhaps a little more satisfying to a certain young woman?' For the others' benefit, he added, 'Dr Elgin's daughter, gentlemen. Both pretty and persuasive – I prescribed some practical therapy for her, with Chief Officer Carrick assisting.'

A frosty smile twitched to life in the corners of Dobie's mouth. 'I've met her.' He tapped the desk top with one small, hard forefinger. 'You'd be wasting your time in that bay, Carrick. The morning after Elgin disappeared a couple of police frogmen went down. Deacon can tell you the result.'

'Absolute zero.' Chief Inspector Deacon stretched into a slightly more upright position. 'They worked an outward radius from where Elgin's boat was moored, and kept at it until they were sure it was useless. What are you trying to do anyway, Carrick? Cause trouble – or earn some gratitude?' Mild amusement took part of the sting from his words.

Carrick flushed and his lips tightened, but Deacon had risen from his chair before he could reply.

'I've got a post-mortem report that gives me a perfectly understandable cause of death, and a whole set of circumstances which confirms it.' The policeman shook his head. 'That's my part finished, Commander Dobie. Accidents happen, always will.' He stopped, his hand on the door. 'Want a lift back, Commander?'

Commander Dobie shook his head. 'No. I'll look in at your office later.'

'Right.' Deacon went out, closing the door behind him.

There was an awkward silence in the room, then Dr Lonson made a show of gathering up the notes on his desk. 'I'll find my secretary and have her start on this. You'll want a copy, Commander?'

Dobie gave a nod. 'Please. Mind if I make a telephone call from here before we go?'

'Help yourself.' Lonson went out, clutching his papers in one hand.

'Paperwork – that reminds me.' Commander Dobie perched himself on the edge of the desk, his short legs swinging free of the floor. 'Got the *Tecta*-incident report ready, Webb?'

Carrick took the envelope from his inside pocket and handed it over, ready for the storm. When the Chief Superintendent of Fisheries seemed quietly friendly, that was the time to take cover.

'I've got to call the department. Bring them up to date on this.' Dobie ran one hand through his thinning hair. 'That won't include telling them you've upset the local constabulary. What's biting you about all of this? There's something out of place, isn't there?'

Slowly, Carrick gave a nod of agreement.

'Then let's hear it, man.' Dobie's legs no longer swung, and there was an underlying bite in his tone. 'Give it an airing. Something to do with the girl?'

'In a way.' Carrick plunged in. 'We talked about her father. According to her, he was a methodical type of man, the type who made sure of every detail. The type who

27

wouldn't panic easily. Would that sort of man, in a really tight spot, forget to release his weight belt? Even if he was passing out, wouldn't he flick it loose, give himself that extra chance to get back to the surface?'

Dobie frowned. It was hard to decide whether the point had scored, or whether anger was gathering. 'That's still not all you're trying to say, is it?'

'Maybe not.' Carrick's face was deliberately expressionless. 'But I'd like to find out one or two things for myself before –'

'Before you risk making more people than yourself look like damn fools.' Dobie sat silent for a moment. 'All right, supposing I let you try to get this out of your system. What would you do? Take a look under the bay?'

'Later, sir. But it might be an idea to have a talk with the people up at Crosslodge.'

Dobie considered again. '*Marlin* will arrive in harbour at eleven this evening. Captain Shannon has his orders – to refuel, tidy up the *Tecta* case, and then get straight back out. There's trouble building up every minute these damned herring shoals are out in the Firth, you know that – and only *Marlin* here and *Skua* working out of Campbeltown to handle it. For the moment, anyway –'

'You're bringing in more, sir?' Carrick knew the reluctance behind such a decision. Any concentration of fishery cruisers in one area was bound to leave large, unpatrolled gaps on other sections of the sprawling coastline.

'I've ordered *Snapper* down from the Minch. She's small, but useful. If that doesn't do it, the department are already wanting me to have the Navy send *Blackfish* round from the east coast.'

Blackfish . . . that certainly explained why Dobie was restless. *Blackfish* was Royal Navy, an armed minesweeper which was the equivalent to a riot-squad ship, and for the Navy's White Ensign to appear on a scene already occupied by the Blue Ensign of the Fishery Protection Squadron would constitute a slap in the face to all concerned.

Carrick felt bound to protest. 'We can handle things, sir. *Snapper* will be all the help we'll need.'

28

'That's what I told them.' Dobie came down from his perch and walked over to the window. 'We've had five more reports of trouble since dawn, Carrick. One was a Campbeltown seine boat. According to her skipper, a trawler tried to ram her off Sanda Isle. Another was an Irish line-boat. She got into a brawl with a pair of ring-netters, and they chased her off with a clip of rifle bullets.' He took out his cigarettes, lit one, and stared out the window. 'What I'm saying is that your first job now is aboard *Marlin*. But when you've a chance ashore, well, there's some doubt about where *Tecta* picked up Dr Elgin's body in her trawl. Then again, it's a reasonable thing for us to want to make sure that there's no chance of this kind of accident happening again to department staff. Both are Fishery problems, our problems.' He turned, and switched on that gnomish grin. 'Let's find out about these things. You – well, you may have to talk to quite a few people.'

'I'd say that's more than likely, sir.' It amounted to a li-cence to hunt, a licence without challenge. Carrick eyed the commander with a new respect for his crafty diplomacy.

'Then get on with it, Mr Carrick.' Commander Dobie reached for the telephone. 'Any particular question you'll ask, by the way?'

'One, sir. One nobody's bothered to ask so far – was there any reason why Dr Elgin should have died.'

Maybe he'd find out. Maybe he wouldn't. But there was more than a copper-tinted head of hair and a snub nose prompting him to seek an answer. Though – yes, they helped too.

Chapter Two

Finding Clapper Bell was purely a matter of perseverance, and Carrick knew the trail to follow. Three bars in the harbour area yielded no trace of *Marlin*'s bo'sun, but in the fourth, a low-ceilinged, smoke-filled place with dark oak rafters and a brass footrail running the length of the counter, the hunt ended.

Inside the bar, a crush of dockers and shore customers had cleared back towards the entrance. The rest of the long, narrow area was manoeuvring space for two distinct groups. At the far end, clustered watchfully together, stood a party of trawlermen. Some were Norwegians from the *Tecta*, and Carrick placed the rest as from the crew of the breakdown-plagued *Karmona*. Facing them, equally matched in number and openly ready for trouble, a force of local fishermen crowded behind their burly, middle-aged leader, whose combination of red hair and a black patch over one eye gave him an almost piratical appearance. The redhead's thick-soled seaboots were placed astride another man lying moaning on the sawdust floor. An overturned table lay a few feet away, beside a debris of spilled drink and broken glasses.

Between the factions, propped with his back to the bar counter, a freshly drawn beer in one hand, Clapper Bell beamed in anticipation. Even if the big Glasgow-Irishman had cast himself in the role of simple spectator, he was making sure of a ringside view.

'Let's have you, then,' invited the redheaded fisherman, moving a couple of steps nearer to the wavering trawlermen. 'You come here with your ruddy trawlers, sucking up the fish like vacuum cleaners, then throwing your damned weight around ashore –' A growl of agreement from his bitter-faced backers drowned the rest of it.

Cautiously, Carrick eased his way through the fringe and reached *Marlin*'s bo'sun. 'What's going on?' he demanded.

Bell kept his eyes on the potential arena. 'Couple o' *Karmona*'s men wi' a bit too much booze began lookin' for trouble, sir. Happy-face on the deck found it.'

Suddenly, Carrick found himself part of the tinderbox.

'Look over here,' shouted one of the seine-netters, a paunchy, bearded fisherman, faded denim overalls held up by an old Boy Scout belt. 'Fishery snoops –' He pushed his face close to Carrick in a gust of stale whisky. 'Well Mister, we don't need you!' His shout turned attention from the trawlermen for a brief moment – a moment long enough for them. From the far end of the bar, they came forward in a rush and a roar. Two seconds flat, and the battle was under way, fists and seaboots flying.

Paunchy spun round, to meet a hammering blow in the mouth which sent him reeling. Carrick saw the redhead grapple with one of the Norwegians, sending the man flying out of the melee to crash into the wall and lie still. As a chair flew through the air and a bottle smashed somewhere in the middle of the battle, Carrick and Clapper Bell found themselves pinned against the bar by the sheer weight of struggling bodies. Around them, the fight raged in an indiscriminate fury.

'Whose side are we on, sir?' *Marlin*'s bo'sun shouted for advice while he fended off one small, enthusiastic attacker, piston-smacking the flat of his hand under the other man's chin.

'Our own –' Carrick ducked a wildly swung chair leg, tripped the wielder, and next moment found himself face to face with the black eye-patch. The fisherman's fist swung, braking in mid-air but still clipping him on the side of the jaw. 'Sorry, mate,' apologized the redhead as he recognized his opponent. He turned away, and dived back into the struggle.

'Outside, come on!' Carrick weaved to fend off a bottle-

31

arm belonging to one of the trawlermen, felt the blow graze his shoulder, and chopped with his right, landing a hand-edge blow behind the man's ear. Clapper Bell was equally busy. His latest annoyance, a dark-faced, gap-toothed fisherman, had jumped on him from the top of the bar counter. As the man landed on his shoulders, *Marlin*'s bo'sun heaved round, caught him by the waist, and boosted his attacker bodily upwards. The fisherman's skull thumped against one of the low wooden beams, and he fell back on the bar counter, mouth hanging open.

'Are we leavin', sir?' Clapper Bell made it clear he personally was in no hurry.

'Yes – and now!' Carrick side-stepped a struggling two-some and edged out to the fringe of the battle. Clapper gave a last, reluctant glance around, shoved a dazed, stag-gering combatant from his path, then carried out a similar retreat. From the battle's perimeter, they saw the redhead suddenly emerge from beneath two trawlermen, poise, then dive back on top of the pair.

'Leave them to it.' Carrick at last managed to drag his companion doorwards, and out into the cobbled street beyond. They strolled away, the din from within the bar still reaching their ears. Further along, two crammed police cars swept past them, heading towards the trouble spot.

'Ach, it was nice while it lasted.' Clapper Bell's face split in a happy grin. 'And I'll bet a week's pay to a bottle o' beer there'll be plenty more.'

'Tempers getting ragged?' Carrick slowed his pace. *Marlin*'s bo'sun had an uncanny knack of soaking up information with every pint he drank.

'Ragged for certain, sir. There's more than just fish involved now – it's breakin' down into a whole load o' personal feuds, boat feuds, port feuds.'

'Lines against nets, nets against trawls – and every last one of them cursing us for being around, unless we're hauling some of the opposition in out of their way.' Carrick had no illusions about the fishery cruiser's unpopularity in the midst of this boom. The European markets were hun-gry for fish. A different year might have seen the quantities being landed constituting a glut, meaning either dumped catches or selling for fertilizer and pet-food prices. But the buyers were still lining up at the harbour wall, their demand constant, their bidding steady, and it was a time when men who were working almost around the clock, making do with the bare minimum of rest and sleep, found tempers fraying. What was launched as a passing joke could become a deep, harsh-barbed insult.

'Clapper, do you know how much fish they've landed on this coast in the past week?'

The bo'sun scratched his fair, corn-stubble hair. 'The devil of a lot, that's all I know, sir.'

'Just over four thousand tons – four times more than they'd hope to get on a normal peak week's fishing. That means big money all round.'

'Helluva big!' Clapper was visibly impressed. 'Makes a bit o' sense out o' one story I picked up. Did you see that bloke back there – the one stickin' his neck out?'

'The eye-patch?' Carrick saw again the bunched, swinging fist that had braked in mid-air. He'd been very glad it had, too.

'That's the one, sir. Just before they blew up back there, he was talkin' to a couple o' his mates. They were full o' a story about two big seine-netters workin' close inshore near Portpatrick, in broad daylight. A lobster cutter passed 'em close – an' they had their names and registrations covered over. More than that!' His companion gave a grunt of sheer disbelief. 'The crews were wearin' masks!'

Carrick gave a thin whistle of startled interest. 'Seine boats – two of them?'

'That's what they said, sir. Why?'

'Because two seine boats worked the same stunt off Mull last year. Covered-up registrations, masks, working in daylight – the locals chased out after them in launches, and it ended in a pitched battle, boarding parties, the lot. But they got away from them, and then dodged clear of *Snapper* when she tried to round them up. Now *Snapper*'s coming down from the Minch to do an assist patrol – her skipper's going to love to hear this!'

'Eh – what about our own ship, sir?' Clapper Bell thought wistfully of his privilege-enriched quarters aboard *Marlin*, almost wanton luxury by comparison with the cramped, damp bunk he'd been lucky to get aboard the Norwegian trawler.

'*Marlin* comes in tonight. She'll sail again as soon as Captain Shannon has demolished our friend Munsen.' That, Carrick promised himself, was something he wouldn't miss. 'Tell Munsen he's going to have a visitor – and warn our own lads not to wander too far from the quayside. I'm not going to be around for the next few hours – I'm taking the station wagon. I've some places to go and people to see.'

'Something to do with the dead bloke, sir?' Clapper Bell was mildly interested.

'Something to do with the dead bloke,' agreed Carrick. 'You can help by asking a few questions around the harbour. He ran a small boat of his own. I want to know how he rated as a sailor, whether he ever needed help, whether he was liked, the general picture.'

'You mean you think somebody croaked him?'

Nobody had ever put the issue in such straight, simple terms before. In fact, he hadn't even brought it down to that simplicity in his own mind. Carrick's mouth tightened a little.

'Yes, I suppose I do.'

Carrick drove the coast road out of Ayr. The dark-blue Humber's tyres hummed over the bone-dry tarmacadam, past Alloway and the clutter of tourists around Burns's Cottage, that thatched memorial to the ploughman poet who was as often remembered in his home country for his women as his words, then on over the new Brig o' Doon, climbing a little past the fishing village of Dunure with its fringing cliffs and crumbled castle. Crosslodge was another four miles on, a newly metalled tree-lined road leading off from the right, barred by a heavy iron gate and a spattering of PRIVATE – NO ENTRY noticeboards.

A blue-uniformed security guard strolled forward from a small, red-bricked gatehouse set discreetly to one side, took a brief glance at Carrick's warrant card, then waved a hand towards the gatehouse window. An electric motor hummed, and the iron gate swung open.

'We were told you'd be along, sir. Straight on to the administrative block, and ask for John Stark – he's production director.'

'Thanks.' Carrick slid the station wagon into gear and drove forward. Through the rear mirror, he saw the gate swing shut again behind him and the guard already speaking into a telephone mounted to one side of the main pillar. Crosslodge, it appeared, had its own, quietly thorough security pattern.

The trees ended after about three hundred yards. Beyond their foliage barrier, the ribbon of road crossed bare grassland – and ahead, like a great, grey metal balloon, Crosslodge's reactor sphere poised its massive bulk close to the edge of the cliffs. The sphere, 150 feet high, a triumph of welded seams and stress engineering, dwarfed the huddle of single-storey concrete bunkers scattered around its base and shrunk even the slender, windowless pillar of the administrative block a little way beyond to near-pigmy proportions.

Carrick slowed the Humber to a gradual halt as he reached the second gate – a duplicate of the first, the only apparent opening in a fifteen-foot-high metal-barrier fence which curved in a vast semicircle around the nuclear station's landward area. The top three feet of fencing angled outwards, and was twined with barbed wire.

'Chief Officer Carrick?' The inner-gate guard saw the warrant card, signed to his watchmate, and pointed towards the tower. 'You'll find a car park just to the right. Mind signing this book, sir?'

Carrick scribbled his signature on the visitors' book, drove through the opened gate, parked the car, then walked across to the broad main door of the office tower.

Within the concrete cocoon, a major effort had been made to overcome its strictly functional exterior. The floor of the entrance hall was a gay mosaic of coloured marble, subdued overhead lighting picked out the rich colours of the deeply upholstered armchairs reserved for waiting visitors, a vast mural on the theme of power through the ages ran its course round the walls, and a smiling young blond receptionist, pert and pretty, greeted him in a way which must have put a fresh spring into the step of many a tired traveller.

He glanced around the mural while she telephoned. The artist had taken for his theme each stage of man's progress in his acquisition of power, from the dawn of time through sailing ships and early steam engines, to the interplanetary world of the day after tomorrow. Places like Crosslodge would probably seem primitive by then – the faint *ting* as the telephone was replaced brought his attention back to the blonde.

'Mr Stark's secretary will be right along, sir.' She bathed him in the smile again, then returned to the work on her desk. A few moments later, the elevator door in the far corner sighed open, and a girl stepped out. She looked across, and recognition flickered on her face. Carrick remembered her too – the raven-haired girl he'd last seen in the back of the red M.G. saloon as Helen Elgin had been driven from the hospital at Ayr.

She crossed towards him, stiletto heels clacking on the marble. 'Mr Carrick? I'm Shona Bruce, Mr Stark's secretary.' Her voice was warm and friendly, and she spoke with a faint, attractively accentuated drawl. 'He's ready to see you.'

He followed her to the elevator. Shona Bruce was fractionally taller than Helen. She'd changed the yellow sweater for a more formal, pencil-slim wool dress in donkey brown, demure enough for business wear, yet figure-hugging in a way which translated the smooth movement of her hips into a rhythm all their own. She pressed one of the control buttons as they entered, the door closed, and the long dark hair, lightly waved, brushed her shoulders as she turned towards him.

36

'Mind if I say thanks for helping Helen this morning? She told me about it.'

'I saw you leave. You're the friend who is staying with her?' The elevator was small, little more than a capsule, and her perfume was light, yet drawing.

'I'll be there for a spell.' Shona Bruce gave a slight shake of her head. 'It's the kind of time friends are for – Helen and her father were pretty close to one another.'

'You work together here?'

'More or less. Helen is secretary to Dave Dunn, the chief engineer. They've given her the rest of the week off.' The elevator doors opened, and they stepped out into a brightly lit, door-lined corridor. 'This is the top floor. Mr Stark's office is along this way.'

John Stark, production director for Crosslodge, rose from behind his desk as Carrick entered, shook hands, then waved him towards the armchair placed opposite the desk. Stark was a plump little man with a pasty-white moon face, bright eyes sharp behind their heavy spectacle lenses. As Shona Bruce went out, closing the door, he leaned forward on one elbow.

'I've had a telephone message from the Atomic Energy Authority about you, Mr Carrick. Asking me to give you any help you need in connection with Dr Elgin's death. But about the only other thing I know is that the original request came from a commander –' He glanced at the memo pad before him. '– Commander Dobie, of the Fishery Department.' Stark pushed forward the cigarette box on one side of the desk.

'Thanks.' Carrick took one of the cigarettes, accepted a light, and sat back. 'We're still working on the background to what happened. My job is to soak up any and every detail I can, just looking for possibilities.'

Stark appeared surprised. 'I thought that was over and done with. The police contacted me before lunch – said the post mortem showed that some kind of oxygen starvation was the cause of death, and that they'd more or less tied up the matter.'

'They're satisfied it was an accident.' Carrick maintained

the approach of mild professional interest. 'But from the Fishery Department viewpoint, we've still to come up with a complete technical explanation, to find whether this could have been avoided. You'll need someone to continue Dr Elgin's underwater work, won't you?'

'That's definite. And we wouldn't like another accident like the last.' Stark relaxed a little. 'Well, how can I help you?'

'For a start, how far out did these sea-bottom surveys extend? Did he ever complain about difficult conditions?'

Stark's small fat lips pouted in thought. 'Well, he was more in contact with Hinton, our reactor manager, and Dunn, the engineering chief. But if he had been worried, word should have reached me. As for the area, that was pretty much up to him.' He pushed the spectacles slightly higher on his nose. 'Know much about nuclear power?'

'Slightly less than nothing.'

'At least you're honest.' Stark chuckled, the professional secure in his speciality. 'All right, this is a perfectly conventional nuclear reactor station, apart from some design features we like to think put us in a class ahead of most. We use uranium to produce heat, convert the heat to drive turbines, and put roughly half a million kilowatts of electricity into the national grid. No dark secrets – we just don't particularly welcome visitors, because they get in the way. Now to Elgin's role. Part of our process depends on using sea water as a secondary coolant – like a car uses air to cool down the radiator, before the radiator water cools down the car engine. Right?'

Carrick agreed. Put like that it seemed reasonably simple, and the scientific miracles behind the process were – well, probably best left as scientific miracles.

'Good. We take in a hundred and fifty million gallons of cold sea water each day, straight from the Firth of Clyde, push it round our cooling system, then pump it back out again. By then it has been warmed up, really warmed. This place is like a big teakettle in a way, pouring a constant flow of near-to-boiling water into Culzean Bay every twenty-four hours.' Stark gave a shrug. 'I'm not suggesting the result will ever change the Firth of Clyde into a tropical paradise, but we've certainly raised the sea temperature in the immediate vicinity by a few degrees.'

'No radioactivity involved?' The question seemed expected of him.

'None. Or so very little it doesn't matter a hoot – and there's a constant monitor kept at the outlet. But we do gather some liquid radioactive waste from other sources as a matter of routine, a strictly supervised routine. In the same way, wash your hands here, have a shower, pour some discarded chemical down a laboratory drain, dispose of any liquid which has had the slightest chance of contact with contamination, and it all ends up the same way. We process it, dilute it until it is umpteen times below the established safety limits, then discharge it well out to sea through a long-reach pipe. The stuff is already safe before it goes out of here, and sea dispersal completes the job – everything done according to the rules. International rules, Mr Carrick. They were laid down by the International Atomic Energy Agency in Vienna back in '61.'

'But Dr Elgin's job was to make sure the rules were always enough?'

'Partly. But your Fishery Research people are keen to keep track of the effect of a local sea-temperature disturbance on marine life. There's also an obligation in this sort of an operation to keep a constant monitoring and sampling programme in being – safety first, last, and always. You want to hear more about what's required?'

'Please.'

'Then I'll turn you over to the technical boys, Dunn and Hinton.' The small bright eyes focused on his and stayed steady. 'Like to know what I think happened?' As he spoke, Stark pressed the buzzer on his desk and began to rise.

'I'm in the market for theories,' agreed Carrick, getting up from his chair.

'Elgin made some damn-fool mistake down there, that's all. I saw him a few days before it happened, found him wandering along the quayside at Ayr Harbour, muttering to himself and blind to everything around. Walked right past me without knowing I was there. Maybe the man was cracking up – maybe not. But don't blame this station for what happened, Carrick. We're not involved.'

The door had opened. Shona Bruce had caught the last of Stark's opinion, but she showed no reaction.

'Miss Bruce, take Chief Officer Carrick across to the reactor area. Mr Hinton's expecting him – and Mr Dunn should be there about now.'

Carrick said goodbye, and followed her out. As the door closed behind them, the girl shook her head in protest. 'That business about Helen's father cracking up – it's idiotic. He and Stark never got on together anyway.'

'You mean they quarrelled?'

'Stark?' She chuckled. 'I've been his secretary for a year – and he never quarrels. If it's someone higher up he says yes sir. If it's someone lower down, he stabs them in the back three months later. Heaven knows how his wife and family stand him.'

'And the next two on the list, Hinton and Dunn? How do you rate them?'

She hesitated a moment, then gave a shrug. 'All right. Alex Hinton is reactor manager. At the moment he's second-in-command to Stark – the deputy director was transferred about three months back, and there's been no replacement. He's a Londoner, the middle-aged, ball-of-fire type. It can be wearing.'

'Married?'

'A bachelor. That's probably half his trouble.'

He followed her out to the elevator. On the way down he brought her back to the subject. 'What about Dunn, the chief engineer?'

'Dave Dunn?' She took longer to decide. 'He keeps pretty much to himself. People say he has a first-class technical brain. Helen says he's considerate and keeps his hands from wandering – the basic priorities. He has a wife somewhere, but that's about all I know. That's about all anybody knows.'

They left the elevator, crossed the entrance hall, passed

40

the blond receptionist, then went out of the administrative tower and into the daylight. A chill northeast wind had sprung up, and the girl shivered, then set a fast pace, heading towards the concrete bunkers nestling so disturbingly close to the base of the giant reactor sphere. They stopped at a grey-painted gate, where the duty guard watched as Carrick signed still another visitors' book.

'Badge, sir.' The man stepped forward and pinned a small metal-framed square to the lapel of Carrick's uniform. Shona was already wearing its duplicate, pinned brooch-style to the neck of her dress.

'Radiation-check badges with an unexposed film inset,' she explained. 'Everyone working in or around the reactor area wears them. They're changed and developed daily for radiation fogging.'

'More safety precautions?' He eyed her quizzically.

'They make sense here.' She looked up for a moment at the welded-steel shell, and her face tightened a little. 'Ready?'

They skirted the first low bunker and entered the second. Inside, along a corridor, concealed lighting, central heating, and a humming air conditioner created a scientifically ideal environment which reminded Carrick of a deodorized submarine. She stopped outside a door marked REACTOR MANAGER.

'I'll leave you here.' She made it both a statement of fact and regret. 'Helen said you might be along at the flat later – if you had anything to tell her.'

'I'll be there, tonight about ten,' he told her. 'It'll be my last chance for a couple of days. We're sailing before morning. Blame the fishing fleets – they're keeping us on the hop.'

A sparkle of amusement glinted in her voice. 'I'm a fisherman's daughter, Mr Carrick – and a fisherman's niece. My uncle will be sailing on the same tide tonight. We've got a forty-foot line-boat, the *Rachel C.*'

'Your uncle?' Carrick found the possibility interesting. 'Couldn't be tall, dark-haired, with a moustache – the man driving the car at the hospital today?'

'No.' She reacted as if stung, then what might almost have been panic subsided to a cool caution. 'That was – was someone else. A friend – a friend of Helen's.' She glanced hastily at the small, square-glassed watch on her wrist. 'I'd better get back.'

She left him, walking quickly along the corridor. Carrick fingered the film badge on his lapel, finding it difficult to locate a reason for the sudden alarm he'd seen flicker in her eyes. He gave up with a rueful shrug, turned to the door, knocked, and went in.

Hinton and Dunn might, in other circumstances, have made a good music-hall comedy team. Hinton was lithe, confident, with a receding hairline and a polka-dot bow tie. Dunn was a paunchy, grey, stoop-shouldered man with frayed shirt cuffs and a suit that had forgotten what it was like to be pressed.

The introductions over, Hinton elected himself spokes-man.

'Elgin? A character – though his daughter's damned pretty. Pretty but cold. Good thing they're not all like that, eh Dave?' He winked towards Dunn, who smiled weakly. 'Elgin came here once a week or so – no set routine. We gave him details of volume discharge of diffused liquid waste, microcurie readings, that sort of thing. He kept us supplied with copies of his own findings, and gave us samples for laboratory testing. Every time he came, the place looked like a fish market – smelled like it too!'

'I thought Elgin was the type who preferred to finish a job on his own.' Carrick could imagine how Hinton reached his post as reactor manager. Minimal technical qualifications, maximum personality projection, equally able to handle a tough-minded shop-steward committee or a righteous VIP delegation with the same easy humour. Hintons were valuable men in any modern industrial complex – as valuable and necessary as engineers like Dunn.

'Just couldn't do that part himself, or he'd have tried. Stubborn old bird.' Hinton leaned back in his chair. 'But the equipment involved doesn't grow on trees. Tell him, Dave – you're the technical brain, not me.'

'I'll try.' The underlying bite in Dunn's grunt was lost on his companion. But Carrick sensed that these two men had a mutual tolerance of one another, nothing more. 'The analytical technique is too complex. Elgin could make preliminary investigations, but then he ran into problems of radiochemical analysis. He'd bring us prepared bottom sediment, weed, plankton, molluscs, fish, and we'd run the final tests. We had the specialized laboratory equipment; he hadn't. Is that enough?'

'Enough for me. Had he fallen behind with these monitor checks?'

'A little, but he could have caught up easily enough. Why?'

'He went down alone on that last dive – against normal practice.'

'Because I had to ask his daughter to work late.' Dunn glanced away for a moment. 'Well, I didn't know until then what they'd planned – anyway, there was no rush. He could have waited.'

'Except he wasn't the type,' chipped in Hinton. 'Remember we kept him waiting once for a batch of lab results, Dave? He practically hung round our necks until we produced them – I talked about priorities and pressure, and it just went in one ear and out the other.'

'Who normally went with him on these sampling trips?'

Hinton shrugged. 'Damned if I know, Carrick. Wasn't part of our responsibility.'

'Did he say why he'd fallen behind in his work?'

'Not to me. I didn't even know it had happened.' Hinton dismissed the matter.

'The last time I saw him he started to make some kind of apology about it,' said Dunn slowly. 'All I can remember is he admitted that he was having to let things slide a little. He said it was a temporary state, that he had to take chances as they came.'

'Which is a pretty good motto at any age.' Hinton fingered the wings of his bow tie. 'Anything else we can help you with, Carrick? Sorry we can't give you our special conducted tour of the premises – there's an executive meeting due this afternoon.'

'Just one thing – I'd like to have a look at the coastal boundary of the station, get some sort of an idea where Elgin was working. I may have to do some underwater checking later.'

'Why not?' Hinton glanced towards Dunn. 'Dave, I've still a couple of memos to knock into shape before the meeting –'

'I'll take him.' Dunn rose brusquely from his chair. 'Ready, Carrick?'

They left Hinton, emerged from the bunker, and walked along a narrow footpath which went straight under the shadow of the steel reactor sphere.

'Big, eh?' Being freed from Hinton's company seemed to have a tonic effect on the Crosslodge engineer. He watched while Carrick looked up at the overhead crisscross of welded seams which ran like a mesh net across the sphere's surface. 'It took 2000 tons of prefabricated steel plate to make that sphere. And inside it? Power, Mr Carrick. The same power that's in a nuclear bomb, except that we've got it chained down and double-padlocked.' He gave a growl of unexpected vehemence. 'We show people around here, explain the process, tell them the way nuclear science can help in everything from medicine and engineering to keeping down insects – all at the same time as we're producing the basic power. Then guess their first question! "Can it blow up?"' For Dunn, it amounted to a speech. He grimaced self-consciously, then hurried on along the pathway.

The cliff rocks began about five hundred yards beyond the reactor sphere. Grey granite, and, here and there, a softer red sandstone formed a harsh mixture of sharp, sheer slopes, rough boulders, and smaller debris which extended to the water's edge and beyond. In height, they weren't particularly impressive – around the hundred-foot mark at their maximum. But they were the reason for a broad, concrete-pillared causeway which ran in a gradual

44

curve to shore level, then connected with an equally new quay, the T-shaped head of which was bare and empty, except for a solitary, silent mobile crane.

'Deep-water berth – deep enough for middle-sized coasters, anyway,' said Dunn briefly. 'We move in most of our stuff by sea.'

'Where was Dr Elgin working?'

The engineer pointed north. 'Over there. They found his boat moored in line with that pillar-shaped rock. That's pretty well the outer fringe of the monitoring area.'

Carrick nodded. Probably a certain amount of loose bottom rock and heavy weed, he guessed. 'What about the water pumping stations?'

'In the other direction.' Dunn pointed again. 'That brick building south of the quay is the intake station. The outlet point is another quarter mile down. Reduces the chance of building up a recirculatory pattern.'

'Supposing Elgin was moving around out there, and came in too close to the intake station?' Carrick faced the Crosslodge engineer. 'Could he have been caught up by the intake flow?'

'And been pulled in?' Dunn pondered the possibility. 'No. First of all, there's an underwater safety screen. Then there's a series of fences, to prevent debris and other flotsam being sucked in. After that, we've got filters. Let's put it this way. If somebody really tried to get close to the pump inlets they could probably manage it. But they wouldn't get out again, and the – the blockage would be spotted right away.'

Carrick had one last question for his guide. 'When you spoke to Dr Elgin, did he appear worried about falling behind with the monitoring work?'

Hands deep in the pockets of his baggy trousers, Dunn turned away from the cliffs. 'Not worried – excited, I'd say.'

'Did he give you any idea why?'

'No.' Dunn frowned. 'Well, nothing definite. He asked me if I'd ever heard of vertical migration. I still don't know what he was talking about.'

'Fish eat plankton – things like underwater insects,' said Carrick, dredging back to his Fishery Protection basic training. 'Plankton come up near the surface by day, go down deep by night. Marine biologists call it "vertical migration", but they don't know why it happens.'

'Does it matter?'

'It might, in terms of fishing.'

'Huh.' Dunn was unimpressed. 'Well, if old Elgin was getting close to finding out anything, looks like it's been lost, doesn't it?'

'Unless he kept notes.' Carrick said goodbye and left the engineer. He had a last glimpse of Dunn heading toward the reactor sphere, then found himself back at the first of the gates. The duty guard took the film badge from Carrick's lapel, carefully noted the departure time in the visitors' book, then opened the gate and let him pass.

It was late afternoon when he got back to Ayr. He parked the station wagon outside the harbourmaster's office, went in, made a telephone call to the Fishery Research office, got the answer he'd expected, and within a matter of minutes was back out again with directions from the harbour staff that guided him to where Dr Elgin's boat had been taken.

The boat, a small twelve-foot launch with an inboard petrol engine, was tied a little distance away from a batch of cabin cruisers and other pleasure craft. Carrick climbed down an iron-runged quayside ladder and went aboard.

Elgin's launch was clean and orderly, an inch or so of water lying in the bilges, some unused specimen jars and tools stored in the bow lockers, an old towel and some cleaning rags bundled into the stern compartment. Carrick closed the stern locker, and started back towards the bow. His weight rocked the boat, sending the bilge water flowing from one side to the other, and he stopped suddenly, bent down, and picked up the thin sliver of broken glass which had been washed into view. The glass had a yellow filter-like tint, and he wrapped it in his handkerchief, then pocketed it, his face suddenly hard and thoughtful.

Carrick knew one source of tinted glass of that type and

gauge. It was used in the face plates of most scuba masks – but not in the one Dr Elgin had worn. And Elgin's mask had been unbroken.

Across the harbour, a siren gave a short, warning hoot. A trio of rusty, dark-hulled trawlers were coming in, salt-faded Red Ensigns fluttering at their sterns, their crews already opening up the for'ard fish hatches. Grimsby boats, from their registration letters – and far away from their usual landing ports. Carrick watched as, in ragged line astern, the trio edged slowly past the cluster of drifters and seine-net boats lying close to the harbour entrance. A little way beyond, white froths of water began to churn from the trawlers' sterns and, one by one, they began to manoeuvre in towards the quayside, berthing close to the two trawlers already alongside. A few figures stood around the *Tecta*'s wheelhouse, inspecting the new arrivals, but the *Karmona* lay apparently deserted, only a faint tail of smoke from her galley chimney indicating life aboard.

Five trawler crews in port, and more probably on the way. It could be a busy night for the harbour pubs – and an equally busy one afterwards for the police patrols. Carrick chuckled at the thought, then, after a last look around the launch, climbed back to the quayside.

Near the harbour gates, the fish-buyers were busy. In the middle of their circle, a cloth-capped auctioneer was hard at work, an upturned packing case as his temporary rostrum, two white-coated assistants labelling the boxes of fish around him as fast as they were sold.

A happy-faced fisherman pushed his way out of the crowd, lit a cigarette with shaking hands, and began to gravitate in the direction of town.

'Good sale?' asked Carrick.

The man's wide, dazed eyes took in Carrick's uniform, and a grin bubbled on his lips. 'Thirty-five shillin' for herrin', seventy-two for whitefish – and we were so full comin' back, the deck was dam' near awash. Dam' near awash, Mister!' He shook his head in joyful disbelief. 'I need a drink, Mister – then my boat's gettin' back out there, back out while it lasts!' He wandered off, rubbing his hands with glee.

Carrick kept on until he reached the *Tecta*. As he came aboard the trawler, Hendrick Munsen's thin, doleful face popped out from the engineroom hatchway.

'Mr Carrick –'

'Skipper?' Carrick waited while the Norwegian scrambled up on deck and came towards him.

'Captain Shannon will be here tonight, like your bo'sun tells me?'

'That's the message I got.'

'Then maybe we can sail, eh?'

'That depends on Captain Shannon,' said Carrick. 'I'll give you one piece of advice, Skipper. Don't try to pull a fast one on him. He doesn't like it, doesn't like it at all.'

'And my fish?' Munsen spread his hands appealingly. 'Two hun'red boxes of fish there are in my holds. Even with the ice and the freezing, they will not keep forever.'

Carrick shook his head. 'I can't let you land them. Sorry, Skipper, but that's the rule.'

'Okay, Mr Carrick.' Munsen shrugged his thin shoulders. 'But soon there will be one dam' fine smell aroun' here. An' two of my crew in jail over some crazy fight in a bar, with the police telling me they stay there till morning – Mamma says we should never have come to this coast.'

'Maybe Mamma's right,' said Carrick sympathetically. 'Where is she?'

'Shopping. For a hat.' Munsen sighed at this final blow. 'You look for your men? They are in the galley.'

Carrick went aft, dodging his way past the coiled trawl ropes and neatly stowed nets. The *Tecta*'s galley was at the stern, the galley door was open, and he looked in to find Clapper Bell and the two other *Marlin* seamen seated comfortably round a table, large mugs of mud-brown tea close to hand, Clapper busy dealing from a grease-stained pack of cards.

'Bo'sun –'

The dealer's activities came to a jerking halt. Bell turned

48

in his chair, then scrambled to his feet, one hand scooping and pocketing the small pile of silver beside him.

'Yessir?' A glare jerked his two companions to their feet. 'Just a quiet friendly game to pass the time, sir.'

'Let's talk about it outside.' Carrick waited while the bulky Glasgow-Irishman stowed the pack of cards in an inside pocket, then walked a few paces away from the galley, to the *Tecta*'s stern. 'Did you check on Dr Elgin?'

'All around.' Clapper Bell relaxed, realizing the card game was forgotten. 'Nice old bloke, pretty handy as an amateur sailor, has most of the local boats keeping an eye open for anything unusual in their catches – goes out a trip with them sometimes.'

'And spending quite a bit of time with them recently?'

Marlin's bo'sun nodded. 'Seems so, sir. He was collectin' samples from just about every catch comin' in – told one or two o' the skippers he was workin' on a special project. Was he, sir?'

'Yes.' Carrick felt suddenly tired. It was a clear thirty-six hours since he'd last slept, and his brain was gradually losing the fight to stay awake. 'Did he have any special friends among the local crews?'

Clapper Bell nodded. 'Some bloke called Bruce, sir. He an' his family run a forty-foot, long-line boat, the –'

'The *Rachel C.*'

'You knew about him?' Bell was surprised.

'Not the connection, but I should have guessed, Clapper. Is she out?'

'Sailed this afternoon, sir,' said Bell. 'Eh – like me to get you a mug o' tea, sir?'

'No.' Carrick stifled a yawn. 'I'm going to find an empty bunk somewhere aboard, climb into it, and get my head down for a spell.' He looked at his watch. 'It's nearly five. Give me a shake before eight.'

Chapter Three

It was Mamma Munsen who switched on the light in the cabin and wakened him three hours later. He groaned, rubbed the sleep from his eyes, and sat up in the narrow confines of the borrowed bunk, which normally belonged to the *Tecta*'s engineer.

'Least you don't snore like the man I got.' She winked at him. 'I brought you something to eat, okay?'

'Thanks.' As her substantial shape retreated, his eyes focused on the swathe of new pink tulle and net on her head, then the pair of heavy, one-piece blue overalls and the old, cut-down seaboots below. Helga Munsen might be back in her working rig, but it appeared she wasn't going to be easily parted from her latest purchase. He grinned, then swung out of the bunk and began dressing.

Outside, through the tiny porthole, he could see the night darkness and the lights of the town reflected in the water of the harbour.

A boat engine throbbed somewhere near, and above it came the staccato clang and clatter of shunting trucks in the nearby railway freightyard. Carrick watched the lights for a moment, his lips tightened to a thin, angry line. It seemed peaceful, ordinary, everyday. Yet out there, or in the Firth beyond, somebody knew both how and why Dr Elgin had died. To Carrick, what might have happened was still as shapeless and intangible as sea mist. But sea mist cleared, and the sliver of glass in his pocket was real. Slowly, very slowly, he was beginning to know the questions he should ask. With a little luck, he might yet discover who possessed the answers.

Half an hour later, he left the cabin. A brief word with Clapper Bell at the trawler's gangplank, and he went ashore, collected the station wagon from the parking area, and drove out towards Helen Elgin's home.

The house, a small, contemporary-styled bungalow with a handkerchief-sized strip of garden to the front, was one of a cluster of identical units lining both sides of an avenue off the broad straight of Racecourse Road. He drew the car in to the kerb, checked the house number, then spotted the low shape of an M.G. 1100 lying parked and empty at the house end of the short driveway. Helen Elgin appeared to have company . . . well, why not?

Carrick walked up the crunching gravel path, rang the doorbell, and almost immediately the hall light within snapped to life and Helen Elgin opened the door. She was wearing a full-skirted dress of dark-green watered silk, caught by a broad leather belt with a heavy silver buckle in a way which accentuated her slim waist and ripe figure.

'You're earlier than I expected.' It seemed part accusation. Then she smiled. 'Come on in, Webb.'

He left his hat on the hall table and followed her through to the room beyond. The house was built open-plan style, lounge and dining room merging one with the other and a sliding wooden-frame door leading off to the kitchen. Over by the rustic brick fireplace in the heavily curtained lounge area, glasses in their hands, Shona Bruce and the dark-haired, thin-moustached man he'd glimpsed in the M.G. earlier, rose from their chairs to greet him.

'You've met Shona,' said Helen.

'But not socially. Hello, Webb.' Shona Bruce wore a white shirt-styled nylon blouse, Black Watch tartan slacks, and lightweight tan pigskin brogues. 'Like a drink? Whisky?'

'Thanks – just by itself.' Carrick glanced inquiringly at the dark-haired stranger.

'Peter Blayett.' The man grinned, extended his hand. He had a strong, confident grip, index and forefinger heavily nicotine-stained.

'I've heard about you Fishery Patrol people, but you're the first I've met in the flesh.' The accent was English, the voice loudly cheerful.

'Peter's a – a friend,' said Helen Elgin. 'He came over to see if there was any help I needed.'

'Arrangements, things like that,' explained Blayett. 'But it seems I'm too late.'

'Your car was at the hospital this morning, wasn't it?' asked Carrick.

'The M.G.?' Blayett nodded. 'I'm able to take some time off when I want, and the girls haven't transport of their own.' He brightened as Shona Bruce returned, bringing Carrick's drink. 'Mind refilling mine, Shona?' He winked as she took the glass. 'Then I'll get going. I've got work waiting.'

'At Crosslodge?' Carrick found it hard to place the other man.

'Among the nuclear brigade?' Blayett grimaced. 'Not me. Haven't got the brains.'

'He's in insurance.' Shona Bruce came between them, the refilled glass in her hand. 'Here's your drink, Peter.'

'Thanks.' Blayett took the glass and with his free hand produced a flat fifty-cigarette box from his left-hand pocket. 'Smoke?' He took one after them, then shook his head as Helen Elgin, having lit her own and Shona's from the same table-lighter flame, came towards him. 'Not third light, sweetheart.'

'Superstitious?' Carrick took third, and watched Blayett follow him. It was an old soldier's habit, dying out. First light, went the story, the sniper saw. Second light he aimed, third light he fired.

'Just habit.' Blayett inhaled deeply. 'Well, as I said, I'm going. According to Helen, you'll have things to talk about.'

'Have we? I mean – have you found out anything, Webb?' She turned towards Carrick, her snub-nosed face suddenly intent.

'There's a – possibility beginning to emerge,' said Carrick.

Blayett glanced at his watch, a gold self-winding model on a plaited hide strap. 'Sorry, I'll need to hear about it later.' He drained his glass. 'Nice meeting you, Carrick – probably see you later. I'll give you a tip. Between them, these two cook a dam' good meal.'

'We'll see you out,' said Helen quickly. 'Webb, fix yourself another drink if you'd like it.'

He nodded. The two girls went out with Blayett, he heard the front door open, the crunch of feet on the gravel outside, then, after a moment, the car's engine start. As it drove away, the front door closed again and the girls returned together. They made quite a pair, he decided. Each strikingly different in looks and personality, Shona dark and coolly attractive, Helen with that warmer vivacity that matched the auburn highlights in her hair. Then his mind clicked to a momentary halt. It wasn't just a trick of the light. Peter Blayett might be Helen Elgin's claim, as he'd been told. But it was Shona's lipstick which was slightly smudged.

That he'd noticed seemed to register with her. The dark-haired girl flushed, picked up Blayett's empty glass, and turned away. 'I'll put this in the kitchen,' she said.

'Webb –' Helen unconsciously bridged the awkward gap – 'you said there was a "possibility".'

Carrick nodded, pushing the other problem aside. 'It's not pleasant.'

'But I want to hear it.' Her face was pale but intent. 'Webb, I had nearly two weeks to get used to the fact that my father was dead and that sooner or later his body would be found. Today was – well, almost a relief.'

He found it easy to understand. 'Helen, how much did you know about your father's work?'

'Most things. Why?'

'He'd fallen behind in his routine surveys, and hinted he was working on another project. I checked with Fishery Research headquarters by telephone – they say it must have been a private project, that they've no record of it. Do you know what it was?'

She shook her head. 'No. I used to type most of his

reports for him, in my spare time. But there was nothing unusual.'

'He worked from here?'

'Most of the time, yes. He was sent here because of Crosslodge, and we fitted up one of the bedrooms as an office.' She was puzzled. 'Why, Webb?'

He took the handkerchief from his pocket, and showed her the splinter of glass. 'I found this on his boat, Helen. Has any other frogman used that boat lately – anyone who might have broken their face-mask glass?'

She moistened her lips. 'No. Shona and I are the only others who've been in the boat . . . and Shona's uncle. He used to crew the boat when he wasn't out on the fishing grounds.'

'What about Uncle John?' Shona Bruce came in as they spoke. Her lipstick had been repaired, and she was once again her confident self.

'Can he use scuba gear?'

'My uncle?' She gave a chuckle at the thought. 'Not likely. You wouldn't ask if you knew him, Webb. He's still not convinced that engines are better than sail. He's a stubborn, red-haired –'

'Red-haired? With an eye-patch and a fighting disposition?'

'That's him,' she sighed.

'Then we've met,' agreed Carrick, rubbing his jaw reminiscently. 'Shona, I've been told that he took Helen's father on one or two trips lately, trips on the *Rachel C*. Did you know about them?'

'Yes. They were just ordinary fishing trips as far as I know.'

'Father went out like that every so often,' agreed the other girl. 'But Webb – that piece of glass. You mean . . .' She bit her lip and didn't finish.

'I mean he may have been murdered,' Webb said quietly.

Shona Bruce gave a gasp. But Helen Elgin's reaction was different, surprisingly different.

'I've wanted someone to say that – say it first,' she said, her voice barely a whisper. 'I thought – but that doesn't matter. I just couldn't see it as an accident.' She gave a faint smile to her friend. 'No, I didn't tell you, Shona. I didn't tell anyone. Would it have made sense?'

'And the police?' Shona asked. 'What do they say?'

'They've decided it was an accident,' said Carrick. 'Don't blame them for that. I've simply been playing a hunch, a hunch that is starting to pay off. Helen, how was your father's launch brought back to harbour?'

'The police towed it in.' She spoke with an iron-like control.

'What was taken from it?'

'Just clothes – the clothes he'd been wearing before he changed into the underwater gear.'

'Nothing else? The engine crank handle?'

'No.' She stared into the fire. 'Does it matter?'

'It matters – when the crank handle, the only way of starting that engine in the first place, is missing and somebody's face mask was broken, broken the way it might have been in a struggle.'

'I – see.'

'Would you show me his office?'

She nodded. They followed her through the house to a large back room, where a laboratory bench occupied most of one wall, flanked by shelves and cupboards laden with specimen jars and other equipment. A roll-top desk stood in one corner, and the window had an undrawn blind in place of curtains.

'Do you mind?' Carrick went over and began searching through the desk drawers. Carbon copies of reports, filed letters, stationery, receipted bills – Dr Elgin's passion for order showed throughout. 'Did he keep a diary, a personal record of any kind?'

'Not a diary, just this –' Helen Elgin took down a large black-covered loose-leaf notebook from one of the shelves. 'It's what he called his work book.'

Carrick turned over the ink-dated pages until he reached the month of October. Then he began to read. Behind him, Shona Bruce lit a cigarette, gave it to Helen, then took another for herself. They stayed silent until, with a shake of his head, he closed the book and laid it down.

'Well?' Helen Elgin puffed nervously on her cigarette. 'Does it help?'

'In a way.' He hesitated, plagued by a sudden sensation that something had moved outside, unsure whether he'd really seen or heard anything. His face hardened to a thin, bitter smile. 'In a way I almost expected, Helen. There isn't a single entry for the ten days before your father vanished. Either he didn't have time to write up his notes, or the pages have been removed.'

She laid down the cigarette, opened the book, and checked for herself. 'But he always wrote them – last thing every night. Always.'

'Webb –' Shona Bruce put her hand on his arm. 'What do we do about it?'

The flicker of movement outside the window was slight, barely registering, but it was enough.

'Go back through to the other room,' he told them. 'We'll talk about it there.' He shepherded them towards the door, put out the light, and followed them.

'Now look, Webb –' Shona Bruce spoke again.

'Not yet,' he told her softly. 'Both of you stay there. Start talking – loudly, about anything.'

She blinked, then understood. 'Helen, what are you going to do about this house?'

Helen Elgin swallowed hard and followed the lead. 'I don't want to sell it just yet, but . . .'

Carrick moved quickly and quietly. He could still hear them talking as he reached the hallway, gently opened the front door, and, avoiding the telltale gravel path, keeping close to the wall and the soft earth of the flowerbeds, reached the rear of the house. Slowly, he edged forward until he could see along the back wall. The curtained lounge windows were about ten feet distant, he could hear the two girls talking, and a figure was crouched below the window level, listening. The eavesdropper was small, fat, and his face a mere dim blob in the clouded moonlight.

Gently, carefully, Carrick took one step from his cover,

then another. Then, as he gathered himself for the dive forward, a hoarse shout came from somewhere behind him. The fat man turned, gave a squeal of fright, and started to get to his feet as Carrick dived towards him. They fell together, the little man kicking, struggling, gasping as he fought. Carrick levered him round with an armlock, suddenly aware of another figure rushing towards them from the dark shelter of the bushes. As the new arrival swung a heavy boot at his stomach, Carrick jerked the eavesdropper still further round, heard the man howl as the blow took him in the back, then wriggled to try to dodge the downward curve of the short, thick cosh in the second man's hand. The blow grazed across his temple and he fell back, making a last grab towards the attacker. He missed, felt his fingers claw instead across the smaller man's head, then the cosh swung again and blind pain scorched through his head.

Light suddenly came streaming out from the house as the curtains behind him jerked open. He heard both girls shouting, and next moment his attackers were running. He lay there, dazed, staring down at his hand in disbelief.

He was clutching a mass of hair, torn straight out by the roots. Yet his fingers had done little more than rake lightly across the fat man's head!

He was still there, still staring, when the two girls reached him.

Marlin arrived in harbour at 2300 hours as scheduled, and Webb Carrick was on the quayside to see her slim grey shape come quietly out of the night and moor beneath a bright pool of dockside lights. She had her choice of berths – the nitrate ship had sailed under ballast, only a handful of fishing boats remained, and even the antiquated *Karmona* had gone, though whether this time she'd manage to reach the fishing grounds and begin trawling had become a dockside joke.

There was time to wait while *Marlin* manoeuvred in, time to isolate in his mind the events of the past hour. For

57

a start, once they'd found him still relatively in one piece, he'd had to fight off the ministering efforts of both girls.

The police? He'd decided against contacting them. Instead, he'd telephoned Commander Dobie, located the Chief Superintendent of Fisheries at home, and had brought him up to date. Dobie's reaction had paralleled his own. '– we're nibbling at something, Carrick, though the devil only knows what. Send me on that splinter of glass, and keep quiet about the rest. If these two young women would feel safer, leave one of your lads with them as a watchdog. Meantime, I'll start a little discreet asking around on my own.'

The receiver was down before Carrick realized there was one item he hadn't mentioned. The handful of hair, sealed in a specimen envelope borrowed from Dr Elgin's room, was a puzzle on its own. A mousey, nondescript brown in colour, greasy, pulled out by the roots, it was a clump thick enough to have occupied close on a square inch of the fat prowler's head. How had it come free so easily? A chronic scalp condition might be the answer. All Carrick knew was that once he'd put the envelope in his pocket he'd suddenly felt unclean and had made a point of washing his hands.

A house guard? Helen and Shona had turned down Dobie's suggestion.

'Not for me,' declared Helen Elgin, her lips parting in amusement. 'Anyway, Webb, have you any idea what it would be like to dump a poor innocent sailor into a house with us? He'd be tangled among wet nylons in the bathroom, be in the way in the kitchen –'

'Even accepting you can produce a poor innocent sailor, Helen's right,' agreed her companion with a matching twinkle. 'We're big girls now, Webb. We can look after ourselves. And what about the neighbours?' Then, more seriously, 'Look, if these thugs wanted to get into the house there's been plenty of opportunity lately – half the time there's been nobody at home. If they had a job to do, something connected with Helen's father, isn't it more likely it was to find out why you were here?'

It had made sense, and he hadn't pressed the idea of a resident guard. He'd gone out with a torch and looked around the garden, finding only a few faint traces of footmarks. Then, after a further, equally negative search through Dr Elgin's room and the dead man's more personal possessions, it had been time to return to the harbour and *Marlin*.

Helen saw him to the door.

'Webb, how long will this patrol last?' She leaned back against the open door, her face shadowed by the angled light from within the house, the result a merciless exposure of the underlying tension she was battling against. 'What's going to happen next – about all this, I mean?'

'It's hard to say.' That was true – a day or a week, even longer, *Marlin* operated to no schedule except her captain's choice and the radio messages which reached out their calls to her. 'But that doesn't mean this goes into deep-freeze, Helen. Other people are involved in this now, people like Commander Dobie.'

She nodded. 'I know.' She had to stand on tiptoe for the quick kiss she gave him. Carrick felt her lips touch his, soft and warm, her body brush against him, then the momentary contact had ended. 'That's just to say thanks.'

Carrick felt a swift, sweeping urge to reach out for her, to hold that slim, ripe body close, search against the curve of her mouth. But then Shona Bruce appeared behind them, and the chance, if it existed, was gone.

'Any more trouble, and let Dobie know right away,' he told them. 'Then, there's always your friend Blayett – it might be useful to have an insurance man around.'

'Peter?' It was Shona Bruce who answered, flushing slightly. 'He – he's out of town quite a lot . . . Helen's never sure when she'll see him.'

Helen Elgin had hesitated for a second before she nodded agreement.

They'd still been standing in the doorway, watching, linked by their very silence, as he'd driven off.

Once *Marlin* had secured, Carrick went aboard and headed straight for the bridge and Captain Shannon.

'Returned to the fold, eh?' Shannon gave his first mate a grunt of welcome. 'Got everybody ready over at the *Tecta*?' The fishery cruiser's commander, a ruddy-hued sixty-year-old, bald and bearded, had only a handful of years to go before he'd be compulsorily retired from the service. That was regulations – and it would be a waste, Carrick knew. Captain Shannon ran a tight ship, could inspire justified terror in newly joined juniors, but knew his coastal waters and his fishermen like few others in the protection squadron.

'All ready and waiting, sir,' Carrick agreed.

'Hmm.' Shannon noted the incipient red swelling on Carrick's left temple. 'I got a signal from Commander Dobie about you, Mister. Can't find enough trouble afloat, is that it?' He picked up his old, battered briefcase from beside the compass binnacle. 'Well, I want to be out of here before midnight – you can tell me about it later.'

Carrick followed him from the bridge to the deck and ashore, where young Jumbo Wills, the second mate, was already supervising the running out of *Marlin*'s refuelling hoses. Wills turned towards them expectantly, but Shannon barely nodded, sweeping past in a fast, stumping gait.

Aboard the *Tecta*, Clapper Bell had already organized for their arrival. The Munsens' cabin, furnishings rearranged and with extra chairs added, had taken on the air of a miniature courtroom. Brought from the galley, a well-scrubbed table occupied the middle of the cabin. Behind it, ready for *Marlin*'s commander, was Hendrick Munsen's favourite, well-padded, chintz-covered armchair. Two other chairs, plain and wooden, were set opposite for Munsen and his wife, and the Norwegian couple were waiting, faces patient and, for once, expressionless.

Shannon marched in, thumped his briefcase on the table and sat down. Carrick squeezed himself into a space over by the cabin wardrobe, while Clapper Bell closed the cabin door and took up a rigid, silent pose.

'Well, Skipper, anything to say to me?' asked Shannon.

'Better perhaps we wait on you, Captain,' said Munsen warily.

'Better for whom?' Captain Shannon snapped open the briefcase, extracted a thin sheaf of papers, then laid them carefully before him. He took a pencil from his inside pocket, and held it lightly between finger and thumb. 'Exactly where do you think this vessel was positioned when you began trawling last night?'

Hendrick Munsen sucked his long, straggling moustache and glanced at his wife. 'Mamma, you have the chart?'

'I'd be surprised if she hadn't,' said Shannon caustically as Mamma Munsen leaned across from her chair, lifted a neatly rolled chart from the nearest of the quilt-covered bunks, and held it in her hands like some medieval cudgel. 'Well, Mrs Munsen – care to show me?'

She beamed. 'It is a pleasure, Captain.' The chart was spread with a practised wrist movement. 'You see, I 'ave marked. Here, near to Downan Point, Hendrick says he will find fish – so we try. And from there, we go like this.' One pudgy, short-nailed forefinger traced along the chart, fractionally outside the three-mile territorial limit, which she'd thoughtfully reoutlined with thick red crayon. 'Then here, off Bennane Head, is where you stop us.'

Carrick's mouth twitched as he watched. Captain Shannon liked nothing more than this type of verbal tussle and with two games already lost to the Munsens, he wasn't likely to miss any chance of seizing the advantage.

'You're sure? Then what about the chunk of seine net Mr Carrick found in your trawl – and the little matter of fishing without lights, eh?'

Hendrick Munsen spread his hands in innocent apology. 'The net was an accident, Captain. Such things 'appen quickly. As for the lights, it is my carelessness – I forget them.' Then, slyly, he put a question of his own. 'Perhaps the skipper of this seine boat can tell you 'imself where it happened?'

Shannon scowled. 'Perhaps. What do you say?'

'As Mamma has showed you, Captain.' The Norwegian trawlerman was more confident, a player gradually realizing his opponent's half-cloaked inability to complete a threatened checkmate. 'We were a little way outside limits – we would not break the law by coming closer.'

'You wouldn't, would you?' Captain Shannon gripped the pencil until it snapped under the pressure of his irritation. 'All right, Skipper. I won't prolong it. The man whose nets you tore was too busy gathering up what was left to drop a buoy and mark where it happened. You were skating close to the line, very close. You could have been where you say – or, more likely, you were here –' The broken pencil stabbed down inside the red-crayon line. 'That's where our radar placed you, Munsen, and if it was enough on its own I'd have you in court, with your boat tied up here until it became part of the accepted scenery.'

'But you can't?' Mamma Munsen gave a hoarse, for once too quickly, confident chuckle.

'No, I can't.' Shannon's face turned an even ruddier hue, which spread until it reached the white of his shirt collar. 'But there are the other matters. Mr Carrick –'

'Sir?'

'What's the rule when a foreign-registered trawler is found fishing within the Firth of Clyde prohibited area?'

'Ports are advised that no fish landings are to be allowed for a period of two months, sir.'

'As Superintendent of Fisheries I'm so advising as far as the *Tecta* is concerned, Skipper. Any queries? Do you wish to appeal?'

Munsen shook his head, unimpressed. 'We did not come to land and sell to Scottish buyers, Captain. What we catch, we take to the German market.'

But Shannon wasn't finished. 'I estimate the damage

done to the seine nets at sixty pounds. There was also a loss of earnings, to be taken into account when compensation is paid. You'll agree?'

The Norwegian's mouth opened to protest, then, as his wife's elbow dug into his ribs, he gulped and nodded.

'Which leaves just one little matter,' purred Shannon. 'Fishing without lights. Mr Carrick, would you say this was a serious case?'

'Particularly serious, sir.' Carrick took his cue. 'They were close to a main navigation channel.'

'Very serious.' Shannon saw the Munsens were worried, which to him meant a moment of minor joy. 'But I've a kind heart, Skipper. Everyone knows that. You'll pay the compensation. You're banned from landing catches for two months. I'm going to – to hold over this other charge. And Munsen, if this trawler as much as empties garbage over the side in the wrong place from now on, I'm going to come and get you. Your ship will be arrested, and what follows will be slow – very slow, understand?'

The trawler skipper was momentarily speechless, but Mamma Munsen's mouth twisted, first with anger, then with resigned good humour. 'Captain –'

Shannon raised an eyebrow.

'Next time we find somebody in our trawl, I hope it is not you.' Her broken teeth gleamed in the cabin light. 'Because maybe we just dump you straight back in again. But now can we sail?'

'Once your husband has signed the compensation agreement. A lawyer will take care of that in the morning, Skipper.'

'Okay, we do that.' Hendrick Munsen chewed on his moustache, none of his wife's humour in the glare he cast around. 'Now maybe you get to hell off my ship, Captain Shannon?'

The magnanimous victor, the Superintendent of Fisheries glanced towards Clapper Bell. 'Bo'sun, you heard. Any of our crew still aboard this vessel will return to *Marlin*.'

'Aye, aye, sir.' Chief Petty Officer Bell saluted, spun on his heel, and went out.

Unhurriedly, Shannon returned the papers to his briefcase. Then he rose. 'Let's not keep these good people back, Mr Carrick. I've a feeling they may have things to talk about.'

Outside the cabin, Shannon closed the door, then put a finger to his lips. After a moment, a loud chant of rage began within as Hendrick Munsen vented his feelings, a chant punctuated by his wife's booming, helpless laughter.

Beard quivering with delight, the Superintendent of Fisheries hopped spryly over the trawler's rail to the quayside.

'Hurry it up, Mister,' he ordered. 'Time the shepherds were back with their flock.'

'Shepherds, sir?' Carrick followed him ashore.

'Yes, shepherds, Mr Carrick. Even though we've got some damned awkward sheep.'

Refuelled and ready, *Marlin* slipped her moorings at 2350 hours. Once clear of the harbour, her commander set a course due west for Pladda Isle, to be followed by a second, southwest leg for the Mull of Kintyre, the southern limit of the long, thin peninsula of land which protected the wide sweep of the Firth of Clyde from the full force of the open Atlantic. The sea calm, with only a slight swell running, the fishery cruiser settled into an easy twenty-knot pace.

'Mr Wills, take over.' As the second mate obeyed, Captain Shannon crooked a finger towards Carrick. 'There's a pot of coffee in the chartroom, Mister. Let's have a talk.'

The coffee was down to lukewarm dregs and a blue haze of cigarette smoke fogged the tiny chartroom by the time Carrick had told his story and had satisfied Shannon's cross-examination.

'Should've taken the boarding party aboard the *Tecta* myself,' growled Shannon at the finish. 'Then maybe I'd have had a share in the fun and games. These two women – good-looking?'

Carrick cupped an expressive thumb and forefinger.

'Hmm. By my age, you prefer steak and chips.' Shannon's manner made it seem unlikely. 'Anyway, you think Dr Elgin was murdered because he'd discovered something – only you don't know how he was murdered or what he'd discovered. Beautifully clear, Mister.'

A brief tap on the chartroom door heralded the radio operator's arrival.

'Midnight weather forecast, sir.' He handed Shannon the typewritten-message flimsy and retired. Shannon glanced at the report, then passed it over without comment.

Digesting the weather summary was, for Carrick, an automatic reflex. Gales in Bailey and Rockall – they were further out on the weather grid, code names for vast areas of the open Atlantic. Hebrides and Malin mattered more. Code area Malin stretched from the northwest coast of Ireland, took in their patrol section, and a lot more besides.

'Wind southwest, force three or four, backing to southeast later and increasing to force seven –' He gave a faint whistle.

'Been building that way for the last twenty-four hours,' said Shannon shortly. 'There's worse out beyond – the weather map looks like a battlefield.'

As seaman to seaman, he didn't need to say more. The sea around *Marlin* might still be calm and peaceful, but somewhere to the west, still at least a day away, maybe even further distant, a foaming cauldron of wind and rain was advancing towards them. For the fishing fleet, the forecast was an ultimatum – stop thinking about your nets, start planning on getting your cockleshells safely home, or take your chance; fine down your safety margin at your own risk, for the sea has no mercy for fools.

'I'm going to get some sleep, Mr Carrick. Call me if I'm needed.' Captain Shannon rose to his feet, more on his mind now than fishing offences or a possibly murdered biologist. If and when the storm broke, he'd be committed to the bridge until it was ended . . . which, in the present, made sleep a precious commodity.

Once *Marlin*'s commander had gone, Carrick lit a cigarette, then went out to the main bridge and joined Jumbo Wills.

'Weather on the way, Jumbo.'

The second mate nodded. 'I heard.' Then, his eyes flickering to the compass and from there to the steering indicator, 'Starboard a point, helmsman.'

'Starboard a point, sir.' The seaman eased the helm round, and *Marlin*'s hull gave a slight shiver as she answered her rudder and eased back on course. Beneath their feet, the deck plates carried the soft, steady throb of the big twin diesels, overlaid by the softer whine of her main dynamo. Above their heads, a crackle of static came from the radio-extension speaker, permanently tuned to the fishing waveband.

From the bridge windows, Carrick could see the whole grey, ghostlike length of the fishery cruiser, picked out by the cloud-filtered moonlight, running in darkened routine, except for her bridge and navigation lights. A duffel-coated lookout was stationed on each of the open bridge wings. For'ard and below, a white-sweatered petty officer stood by the twenty-one-inch searchlight. Aft, to the rear of the squat smokestack, *Marlin*'s motor pinnace was cleared and ready for use.

They made their first contact a mile south of Pladda Isle, the designated end of the first leg of the patrol.

'Fishing boats at three o'clock, sir,' called the starboard lookout.

Carrick picked up the bridge set of 10 × 50 night glasses and focused on the rough bearing. 'I've got them, Jumbo. Four of them – line-boats.' Working for cod and haddock probably, each laying out their great skeins of cord, 200 baited hooks to each 1200-foot line, maybe half a dozen lines per boat. 'Lights okay, everything in order.'

The bridge loudspeaker's static was interrupted, first by a harsher, scraping noise as someone used a fingernail to test a newly activated microphone. Then came a soft whistle, followed by a voice. 'Hello, Charlie, Charlie – Pladda.' Hoarse, steady breathing took over a moment, then the whistler launched into a tuneless version of 'Loch Lomond'. A dozen bars of the ballad, and the loudspeaker fell silent again.

'They're playing our tune,' said Jumbo Wills, listlessly fulfilling time-honoured ritual.

The message had been passed. Thanks to one of the line-boat skippers, every fisherman within range knew that a Protection cruiser was in the Pladda area. Yet the message was too brief to be traced, too apparently meaningless to allow any action.

'Helmsman, I'm going within hailing range.' Carrick had another possibility in mind. 'We'll go ahead of them, to avoid their lines. Take her slow ahead, Mr Wills.'

'Slow ahead, first.' Jumbo Wills fell into the easy formality of ship running. The bridge telegraph rang and was answered, and as *Marlin*'s progress slowed, her bow wave began to curve towards the cluster of fishing boats.

When they were about a hundred yards from the nearest of the line-boats, Carrick took the loud-hailer and thumbed the switch.

'I'm looking for the *Rachel C.*, out of Ayr.' His amplified voice rasped across the water. 'I want to talk to Joe Bruce, her skipper – personal business.'

From the nearest of the line-boats, a speaking horn returned the hail. 'Sorry – he's not around here. Gone further out.'

'Any idea where?'

'I'd like to know myself,' came the fainter reply. 'He's found a good seam of halibut – and he's keeping it to himself.'

'Right – and watch that radio chatter.' Carrick switched off and nodded to Jumbo Wills. 'Continue patrol.'

The second mate gave their helmsman their new course, for the Mull of Kintyre. Then, as *Marlin* gathered speed again he asked, 'What was that about, Webb?'

'Just a hope that didn't come off,' said Carrick briefly.

'Why not raise him on the R.T.?'

Carrick shook his head. Joe Bruce was his main link now with Dr Elgin. The red-haired fisherman seemed more likely to know more about the dead biologist's movements than anyone, and the last thing Carrick wanted to do was to literally broadcast the fact. 'It doesn't matter.' He saw the second mate stifle a yawn, and remembered that for the last twenty-four hours *Marlin* had been down to two watchkeeping officers. 'Get some shut-eye, Jumbo. I'll take the rest of the watch.'

Off the Mull of Kintyre at 0300 hours, *Marlin* passed through a scattering of ring-net drifters and kept on a westerly course, pushing her bow through the deepening Atlantic swell. Then Carrick turned ship, taking the fishery cruiser back in a semicircle which kept clear of the drifters' horizon before setting a new course prowling up the east coast of the Kintyre peninsula. The fishing wave band was beginning to chatter its strange messages from boat to boat and sea to shore, where each skipper's family would have at least one member on duty by the living-room short-wave receiver.

'Tell Ma I'll have breakfast at Aunt Aggie's' . . . 'Plenty o' rabbits, but damn-all hens around here' . . . 'A double row o' buttons' . . . It was a gibberish which carried catch news and market prospects. Few, if any, mentioned the threatened bad weather.

Further north, Carrick spent half an hour shepherding two over-enthusiastic boats out of the North Kilbrannan exercise zone – the Firth could be a busy enough place for British and American submarines on diving practice without some unhappy submariner surfacing into a cocoon of nets.

The stern lights of the two offenders were still disappearing east, and Carrick was considering the possibility of raising sandwiches and coffee from *Marlin*'s galley when he heard footsteps on the companionway behind him.

'Mr Carrick.' Captain Shannon was fully dressed, his

bearded face an odd mixture of anger and disbelief in the dim glow of the bridge lights. 'I'm taking you off watch-keeping as of now. You'll go directly to your cabin. Remain there until further orders.'

'Sir?' Carrick stared at him.

'You're confined to your cabin, Mister – and don't look at me like that. I'm neither mad nor drunk.' Shannon broke off as Jumbo Wills clattered into the bridge, still stuffing his pyjama top into the waist of his uniform trousers. 'Mr Wills – stand clear of the first mate. That's an order. Take over the watch, set course for Ayr harbour, and proceed there at maximum speed.'

'But –' Jumbo Wills dried up under Shannon's glare. 'Aye, aye, sir.

'Mr Carrick.' Shannon jerked his head towards the companionway, and Carrick crossed towards him. *Marlin*'s commander lowered his voice to a rumbling whisper. 'I had a priority radio message ten minutes ago. Personal attention – had to decode the damned thing myself. You're in trouble, Mister.'

'Trouble? Trouble about what?' Carrick had had enough. 'What's going on?'

'Hmm.' Shannon combed his beard with his fingers. 'Well, you've a right to know. Webb, some ruddy fool says you're radioactive, contaminated, hell, you know what I mean. You're to be taken straight to Crosslodge for decontamination – and to tell them how it happened.'

69

Chapter Four

For the second morning running, Carrick watched dawn break over the Ayrshire hills. But this time, his view was restricted to the area bounded by the salt-stained glass circle of his cabin porthole as *Marlin* creamed a bustling path towards harbour. Outside the cabin door, a seaman stood guard – 'not to stop you coming out, but to stop anyone coming in' – was Captain Shannon's tactful explanation.

Once the fishery cruiser had moored, Shannon personally escorted him to the gangway and across the quayside to a waiting ambulance, where Alex Hinton, the Crosslodge reactor manager, stood hunched in a heavy overcoat and shivering in the cold dawn air. Two other men, one carrying a small but heavy suitcase, stood nearby.

'Morning, Captain.' Hinton nodded to Shannon. 'I'll take him over now.'

Captain Shannon scowled. 'How long will this take?'

Hinton gave a shrug, almost lost in the depths of his coat. 'Depends on how serious it is – you know, Carrick, you've caused quite a spot of panic over this.' He thumbed towards the other men. 'I brought two of our technicians, Captain. They'll have to check his quarters and that sort of thing before your ship can sail again, but they'll be as quick as possible.'

Marlin's commander gazed skywards in mute despair.

'Has to be done, I'm sorry.' Hinton gave a comradely smile. 'But not to worry, eh? Ready, Carrick? Next stop – well, we call it the scrub shop.'

Carrick boarded the ambulance, Hinton swung in after him, the doors closed, and they were off.

'What's it all about?' Carrick had been asking himself that one question for the last three hours.

'Simple.' Hinton handed him a cigarette, lit one himself, then tossed over the matches. 'Keep them – they'll probably be destroyed later.' He puffed on his cigarette, and blew the smoke towards the ambulance ventilator. 'When the laboratory developed the radiation film badge you wore yesterday, the negative was completely fogged. They called John Stark – as production director, he's nominally responsible for security, such as it is – he started the wheels turning, and I drew the job of collecting you. What happens next depends on what size of dose you've copped.'

'Thanks very much,' said Carrick grimly. 'Mind telling me where this happened?'

Hinton eyed him strangely. 'We were rather hoping it would be you who'd tell us, Carrick. Your badge was the only one in the whole plant which showed any sign of fogging. Stark wants to know if you were doing some private exploration. Eh – just for interest, were you?'

'Maybe.' Carrick answered shortly, gripping the ambulance's bench as the vehicle cornered.

'That's all?' Disappointed, Hinton pursed his lips. 'Well, take a tip, friend. You'd better have your story ready. John Stark regards Crosslodge as private property. Mentioning it and radiation leakage in the same breath is blasphemy in his book.'

Carrick didn't answer. An alarm signal had begun ringing in his mind, an alarm which traced its way back to a time before he'd visited Crosslodge. But first, he had to be sure. . .

'The scrub shop' at Crosslodge, the nuclear station's Bio-Health Unit, was stationed in one of the blockhouse buildings. It was a white-tiled place of sterile, filtered air, its compartments divided one from the other by rubber-sealed double doors, and Dr Morden, its supervisor, was ready for Carrick's arrival.

'First you strip, then we take a reading,' explained the young, freckle-faced medical specialist as they stood in the outer treatment room. He grinned towards a buxom, middle-aged nurse in the background, who wore the duplicate of his own yellow protective clothing. 'Don't worry about Mary. You'll be so much walking meat to her.'

Carrick undressed, put his clothes in the indicated plastic bin, and followed them through the first set of double doors. Beyond, most of one half of the next room was occupied by a broad, seven-foot-high bank of cream-panelled, dial-encrusted equipment. There was a footplate before it and two fist-sized holes in its face.

'Feet on the plate, hands in the slots, please.' Morden threw a switch and Carrick saw a needle rise. A buzzer gave a shrill squawk.

'Radiation monitor – a fancied-up Geiger counter,' explained Morden, checking the reading. 'Well, you're hot, but you're a long way off cooking.' Carrick stepped down, and a smaller, hand-held instrument was passed slowly across his body. The doctor eyed him seriously. 'Don't suppose you'd like to be shaved, Mr Carrick. Head to toe, I mean.'

'Not if I can avoid it,' agreed Carrick fervently, suddenly very conscious of his nakedness.

'We'll see.' Morden was doubtful. 'There's a shower cabinet next door. Soap, water, and an old-fashioned scrubbing brush. That's first-stage treatment – the rest is up to you.'

Carrick soaped and scrubbed for twenty minutes, dried off, came out, and returned to the monitor. Once again its buzzer gave a high-pitched squawk.

'Again, Mr Carrick.'

At the end of the second scrub, his skin was pink and sore. But the buzzer's squawk was more subdued, and his freckle-faced tormentor nodded satisfaction over the needle readings. 'Put away the razor, Mary. Once more should do it.'

Carrick scrubbed on until every inch of skin was howling its individual torment, and this time the monitor buzzer was silent. There was still a faint trace of radiation on his left hand, but the Bio-Health team's standards were satisfied.

'We'll give you a surgical glove for that hand – wear it when you're eating or handling food,' said Morden. 'Mary'll give you some overalls and other clobber to wear for the time being.'

'What about my clothes?' Carrick gratefully began pulling on the bundle of fresh-laundered garments which the nurse had produced.

'No promises, but we'll salvage what we can.'

'There's an envelope in one pocket,' said Carrick. 'Whatever else you have to destroy, make sure it's kept.' As the other man nodded, he asked, 'How bad was this?'

'Mild.' The Crosslodge doctor unzipped his protective suit. 'Personally, I'd say you've been in contact with some medium-level source of radiation. You picked up a sixty-roentgen dose on your hands, with minor contamination spreading from there. I wouldn't worry about secondary contacts, people you've met since – but the primary source is a different matter. What happened?'

'Mind if I ask a couple of questions first? If this – this source had been in sea water for some time, would it still be active? And suppose somebody got a heavier dose, how would it affect them?' A lot depended on the answers.

'Sea water would dilute the concentration, but wouldn't affect the immediate radiation life of what remained,' said Morden. 'It's hard to be specific without knowing circumstances.' He rubbed his chin. 'A heavier dose? Well, the result would be radiation sickness – growing weakness, lassitude, complexion darkening due to pigmentation side effects, blood-cell damage, hair beginning to fall out. Any or all of them, depending on half a hundred factors.'

The answers fitted, fitted all the way. 'I told you about an envelope,' said Carrick grimly. 'Inside it you'll find a clump of human hair. Try it on your monitors, Doctor. See what they say about it, and you may get a surprise. There's another item I'd like you to sample – but first, I want to see John Stark. Can you fix it for me?'

'You couldn't avoid seeing him if you tried,' Morden grimaced. 'He's waiting for you now, over at administration.'

Four faces turned towards Carrick as he entered the production director's office, four faces each to some extent reflecting their owners moods.

John Stark was angry. His small, sharp eyes glittered wrathfully through their heavy spectacle lenses as he sat primly behind his desk. Alex Hinton stood beside him, watchful, a slight, cynical twist to his mouth. David Dunn was also standing, his back to a multicoloured wall chart, his tie off centre, his manner one of puzzled concern. But the fourth figure in the room gave Carrick his biggest surprise. Commander Dobie sat relaxed, almost sleepily, in the armchair placed to one side of Stark's desk, and the Chief Superintendent of Fisheries gave the faintest of winks towards his junior officer. The message seemed clear. Play it carefully, but don't worry, you're not on your own. . .

Stark cleared his throat, a forced bark which demanded attention. 'I've just had the Health Unit on the telephone, Carrick. They say you're clean –'

'In more ways than one,' murmured Hinton softly.

The production director's small, fleshy nostrils flared at the interruption, his voice became a harsh staccato. 'They say you're clean, Carrick. You've been lucky. But we're not fools. You went poking around on your own when you were here yesterday, didn't you? Poking around after Dunn had left you, poking around like a fool – almost as big a fool as Dunn was for not escorting you all the way back to the exit point.'

Dunn stared down at the floor in silence as the outburst ended, but Commander Dobie's reaction was very different.

'Don't judge too quickly, Stark,' he said brusquely. 'Now's as good a time as any to say it – whatever Chief Officer Carrick has done, he has done while carrying out orders.' As Stark's mouth hung slack with surprise, Dobie turned away from him. 'What's your own explanation, Carrick?'

'No explanation, sir – a suggestion.' Carrick measured his words carefully. 'If Dr Elgin's scuba gear is examined, I think you'll find it is radiation contaminated – and that any contamination found on me was the result of handling that gear.'

'Good, very good,' said Dobie, with all the quiet pleasure of an examiner whose student candidate has fulfilled expectation. 'Mr Stark, you'll find the entire outfit in the back of my car. No need to worry about the car – I had the gear placed in a suitable container.' He gave a flickering smile. 'No magic, Chief Officer. Just logic once I was told you were – ah – unclean.'

'But – but this is madness, sheer madness.' Stark at last found his voice. 'You're dragging back the ridiculous notion that Elgin's accident involved this power station –'

'Wrong word, Mr Stark, Elgin's murder.' Carrick crossed over to the production director's desk. 'If you're so sure this is madness, there's an easy way to prove it.'

There was a moment's silence in the room while Stark sucked hard on his lips and turned towards his two subordinates for their reactions. Hinton, his face expressionless, gave a slow nod of his head. Dunn had the air of a man both dazed and tired.

'All right.' Unconvinced, but wavering, Stark reached out and pressed the intercom switch on his desk. 'Miss Bruce, come in please.'

Not another word was said until Shona Bruce appeared. She glanced quickly at Carrick, then just as quickly looked away again.

'Miss Bruce, contact the Health Unit and tell them I want a full series of radiation tests carried out on –' Stark swallowed his reluctance – 'on the underwater equipment they'll find in Commander Dobie's car.'

'They'll need these,' said Dobie, sliding his car keys across the desk.

'Thank you.' Stark passed the keys to his secretary. 'Tell Dr Morden I want the results immediately.' He gave a scowl as she hesitated. 'That's all, Miss Bruce.'

'Mr Stark, is it –'

He cut her short. 'I said immediately!'

Shona Bruce nodded, turned, and went out. The door closing behind her seemed to act like a signal, freeing Dave Dunn from his verbal paralysis.

'You're seriously asking us to believe this? Without reasons, against all the evidence –'

'With reasons and with evidence,' Carrick corrected him, saw Dobie shake his head in a quick warning, and said no more.

'So what do we do while we're waiting?' mused Hinton, serious for once. 'Sit and look at each other? If there is a radiation reading on the frog suit, how did Dr Elgin stray into contamination?' He cocked his head towards the Crosslodge engineer. 'Dave, you're sure of these outlet filters? I mean – well, accidents can happen. Remember the Windscale accidents . . .'

'There's been no radiation leakage from this station – I can guarantee it.' John Stark squashed the suggestion. 'I've spent most of the night checking inspection records. All monitors are functioning. Elgin's own reports show off-shore conditions are normal.'

'But Elgin was behind in his reports,' said Commander Dobie. 'And we're talking about murder, gentlemen. Not an accident.'

'Elgin wouldn't have been alone on the night he disappeared, if his daughter hadn't had to work late,' Carrick paused, letting the words sink in. 'Mr Dunn, why did you ask her to work that night?'

'Because – because she's my secretary,' said Dunn, startled. 'I needed her at a meeting.'

'Who else was there?'

'I was,' said Hinton from the corner. He chuckled. 'Don't worry, Dave. I'll be your alibi. We met in my office – Dave and I, with Helen taking notes. My own secretary was on sick leave. We worked until after ten, then broke up and went home, straight home.' He spread his hands triumphantly. 'Of course, you can always suggest that Dave or I nipped out of the room for five minutes, took a quick swim out into the bay, tapped old Elgin on the head, then came straight back in to work again.'

'Mr Hinton, don't act the fool.' Commander Dobie's voice slashed across the room. 'What was the reason for this meeting? Who asked for it?'

Hinton flushed. 'Well . . . Dave did, I suppose. He phoned me late in the afternoon.'

Dunn nodded. 'That's correct.'

'What was so important about this meeting that it had to be the same evening?' asked Carrick.

'Now look here!' John Stark shot upright from his chair. 'There's been enough of this –'

'Sit down, Mr Stark,' said Commander Dobie softly. 'Sit down and be quiet.' The little ex-m.t.b. commander held Stark's gaze with his own, beat it down, and Stark slowly subsided.

'The meeting was my idea,' said Dunn hoarsely. 'Alex Hinton is responsible for labour relations, and I had some staff problems. He'd been wanting to get them sorted out, but I'd never been able to find the time. So – so I suggested the one way I could make the time was by having the meeting in the evening.' He gave a helpless shrug. 'The meeting was no secret. I suppose quite a few people knew it was scheduled.'

There was a long silence in the room, a silence none seemed willing to break.

'Damned if I like a room without windows,' said Commander Dobie conversationally. 'Reminds me too much of a blasted beehive.' He broke off as the intercom buzzed. Stark pressed the answer switch with anxious speed.

'Dr Morden from the Health Unit, sir,' announced Shona Bruce's voice.

'Send him in.' Stark released the switch. A globule of perspiration ran down his forehead and he brushed it aside; Stark was worried, worried stiff . . . for himself, for Crosslodge's reputation, or for both?

Dr Morden came into the room, glancing round the gathering, stopping awkwardly and uncertain a few paces from Stark's desk.

'You've completed the tests?' demanded Stark.

'Yes, sir.' Morden's freckled face showed puzzled embarrassment.

'Well?' Stark was in no mood for hesitancy.

'Strong gamma radiation, sir. The concentration varies – up to 200 roentgen in some parts of the inner surface of the suit.' He nodded to Carrick. 'I already said you were lucky. If this is what you were handling, say an extra "thank you" in your prayers tonight.'

'You're sure?' Stark was visibly shaken.

'Sure enough to want a list of everyone who has handled the equipment, sir.'

'Can you identity the initial source?' asked Carrick. 'The type of radiation, how it may have originated?'

'We're working on that, but it takes time,' said the young specialist. 'Mr Stark, I may need additional facilities.'

'You've complete freedom and my personal authorization,' said Stark harshly. 'Requisition what you need.'

'Doctor, what about the other sample?' Carrick felt the palms of his hands moist and sticky, and rubbed them against the overalls. 'Have you checked it?'

Morden blinked. 'The envelope with the hair sample? I wanted to ask you about that. We're finished with your clothes and, well, sorry, but you can't have them back. There's borderline contamination in places, and it isn't worth the risk. But I checked the pockets myself, and there isn't any envelope.'

'You're positive?' The inference hit home like a hammer blow.

'Absolutely.' The young Health Unit man scratched his chin. 'Maybe you left the envelope aboard ship?'

'It was there, in the left-hand pocket of the jacket,' insisted Carrick.

'The left!' Morden found that equally painful. 'We found the main concentration of contamination in that pocket.' He sighed. 'I thought I was being clever when I linked it with your left hand receiving the heavier radiation dose.'

'Hair? An envelope?' Commander Dobie leaned forward in his chair. 'First I've heard of this.'

'One of last night's souvenirs, sir.' Carrick kept his attention on the young specialist. 'How many people would have access to the Unit building?'

'Nearly anyone, I suppose – anyone with access to the reactor zone.'

'And they could have checked through my pockets?'

'Yes.' Dr Morden was consciously out of his depth. 'The outer room would be empty while we were with you at the radiation monitor. But – well, can't you get another hair sample?'

'No.' Carrick gave a bare, lip twist of a smile. 'The owner didn't leave his calling card.'

'He may soon wish he had,' said Morden seriously. 'If the hair represented a separate radiation source, he's in need of treatment, a lot of treatment.' An idea struck him. 'We could always monitor-check the reactor-zone personnel. If they'd been in contact, it would register.'

'Not unless they were pretty stupid,' said Alex Hinton lazily. 'Wear a pair of rubber gloves, ditch them once the job was done, and they'd be in the clear. It could be anybody, even one of us before we came together here.'

'Well, it was just a suggestion.' Morden shrugged, then glanced towards Stark. 'I'd like to get back to work, sir.'

'Go ahead.' Stark sat hunched behind his desk, a man whose load of trouble seemed to be doubling by the minute.

'Hinton, as of now, you and Dunn start a full inspection of this station – monitor systems, reactor plant, the core, uranium stocks, everything. I want a report on any and every irregularity by first thing tomorrow, earlier if possible.' He pushed his pride aside. 'Carrick, I'm sorry for what I said earlier. I'll appreciate your help in giving us a list of people who've contacted Dr Elgin's equipment. I'll organize the rest.'

Carrick nodded. Stark was an organizer by profession, and there was plenty of need for those talents as things stood.

Another problem was troubling the nuclear station's production director. 'Commander, internal security at Crosslodge is my responsibility, just as yours is the sea. But there's the rest –'

Commander Dobie picked up the thread of thought. 'I'll advise the civil police,' he agreed. 'But the next real moves are here, Mr Stark. Until they're accomplished, there's not much anyone outside can do.'

Preparing the 'contact' list was a fairly simple matter. It began with two of the *Tecta*'s Norwegian deck hands and included Petty Officer Bell, the mortuary attendants, and the county police surgeon. Once he'd completed the draft, Carrick left the rest to the Crosslodge unit. They'd have to monitor each and every contact, though there was consolation in Dr Morden's belief that few if any would require more than a cursory inspection.

The meeting broke up. Outside the administration block, Dobie guided Carrick towards his car, a service-blue Ford Zephyr.

'I'll take you back to harbour,' he said. 'But as far as *Marlin*'s concerned, you're temporarily off patrol duties. I've ordered a relief through from base, and he'll take your berth until this is finished. Transfer your kit ashore – and I'm assigning you Petty Officer Bell. He's a handy character to have around.' Dobie's face hardened. 'Stand on other people's corns if you need to, Carrick. You can tap the Fishery force for help at any time, and I'll make sure you find the police friendly. The truth may be here on shore or somewhere at sea. Either way, I want it.'

The drive to the harbour gave Carrick a chance to plan. Two steps seemed paramount, to make his own inspection under the surface of Culzean Bay and to talk to Joe Bruce when the *Rachel C.* returned with its catch. Then there was another matter, one outside his immediate province.

'How would you rate the security screening at Cross-lodge, sir?'

'Reasonably thorough,' said Dobie, his eyes on the road ahead. 'Not the full treatment, because it's a commercial reactor. Thinking of Dunn?'

Carrick shook his head. 'No more than of the others. But somebody, man or woman, took that envelope from my pocket. They may have been looking for something else, but when they saw the envelope they knew that it mattered.'

'Somebody at Crosslodge is tangled up in this,' agreed Dobie, changing gear as he spoke. 'But I can tell you that from the security viewpoint Crosslodge's staff all rate as upright citizens.' He clucked to himself. 'Upright! Lord help us – they're usually the worst of all, and the hardest to nail.'

They reached the harbour at ten a.m. Heavy grey clouds were building up, and a drizzle of rain began sweeping the quayside as the car parked close to *Marlin*'s berth. Across the water, the rusty, down-at-heel *Karmona* was back in yet again . . . fresh trouble seemed to have hit the luckless Irish trawler, and she had moored only a few yards along from the *Tecta*, which showed every sign of preparing for sea.

Commander Dobie led the way aboard *Marlin*. The Crosslodge technicians had finished their task, the fishery cruiser had a clean bill of health, and Captain Shannon was openly impatient to get back on patrol.

'You're taking Carrick – and Bell?' His dislike of the idea was equally unguarded.

'Carrick's relief will be here within the hour,' soothed Dobie. 'I'm giving you Warner – he's a good man.'

'Huh.' Captain Shannon saw no reason for gratitude. 'And Bell? Who replaces him?'

Carrick left them to it. He located Clapper Bell 'tween decks, told him to get ready and have two sets of scuba gear taken ashore, then went to his cabin. It had a rumpled appearance – the Crosslodge technicians hadn't left anything to chance in their radiation check.

Whistling softly, Carrick changed from the borrowed overalls into his spare uniform, packed a few other items into his duffel bag, stowed some of the remaining kit so that his relief would have at least a corner to call his own, then slung the duffel bag on his shoulder and returned to the deck.

A car horn honked. 'Over here, sir –' Clapper Bell was at the wheel of the Fishery Department station wagon, the scuba sets in the rear beside his own much-travelled kit bag.

Carrick acknowledged with a wave, went down the rain-soaked gangway, and stopped beside the car. 'You've got the okay to use this, Clapper?'

'Personal, from Commander Dobie himself,' beamed the Glasgow-Irishman. 'Where do we go first, eh sir?'

'We don't – you do,' Carrick told him. 'Slide along and I'll take you round to the *Tecta*. Get the two Norwegians who handled Dr Elgin's body and bring them ashore.' He glanced across the harbour, saw the ambulance which had newly drawn up beside the trawler, and changed the order. 'Don't bother. Somebody else is taking care of that part. But you're still going for an ambulance ride, Clapper.'

'Me? I'm all right. If it's the radiation thing, those fellas from Crosslodge looked me over 'board ship!' Bell goggled at him, then moved along the wide bench seat. Carrick clambered in out of the drizzle and tossed his duffel bag into the rear of the car.

'Your name's on a list for special attention, and special attention you're going to get. Right?'

'Ach – right, sir. No use startin' a ruddy war over it,' commented Bell gloomily. 'Where do I meet you once the atom squad are finished?'

'The north quay, at Dr Elgin's launch. Bring a starter crank for the engine, regular size, and we'll go on a trip.' Carrick set the Humber in motion.

The drive round the harbour took a couple of minutes. He unloaded his passenger close to the *Tecta*, and saw him begin his reluctant progress through the rain towards the ambulance. Hendrick Munsen was at the trawler's rail, his face a study in gloomy despair as two of his men headed in the same direction. Another sailing delay wasn't calculated to please the Norwegian skipper, and there might be worse if the Crosslodge technicians found any hint of radiation aboard the trawler – or, equally important, among the fish it already had on ice in its holds.

That was Munsen's problem. Carrick chuckled, backed up the Humber in the first stage of a turn, started to change gear, but instead let the car idle in neutral.

Aboard the *Karmona*, moored a bare fifty yards away from him, three men were talking under the small shelter deck beside the engineroom hatchway. One, in oil-stained overalls, he guessed was the trawler's long-suffering engineer. The man beside him also wore overalls, but clean and white, with, on the back, the legend ORBIS FUEL SALES AND SERVICE. The Orbis company service truck was parked a little way off.

But what was Peter Blayett, insurance agent, doing aboard the trawler? Carrick switched off the car's ignition, slid himself further down the seat cushions, and watched.

Neat in a lovat check sports suit, white shirt, and dark tie, Blayett spent about five minutes talking to the two engineers. The conversation seemed friendly enough from that distance, though once or twice the oil-company technician shook his head as the trawler engineer pointed an emphatic finger below deck. Finally, Blayett left them, jumping the narrow gap between trawler deck and quayside with catlike ease. Carrick slid lower in the Humber's seat, but the tall, coatless figure hurried through the rain, passing the car's damp, steamed windows without a glance at its occupant.

Through the rear-vision mirror he followed Blayett's progress until the man turned down the gap between two warehouse sheds. In less than a minute, the red M.G. 1100 nosed out of that same gap and, Blayett at the wheel, drove towards the harbour gates at a gentle second-gear crawl. The view was momentarily blocked as the Crosslodge ambulance pulled away from beside the *Tecta* and took the same route, and when Carrick next saw the red car it had reached the gates and was turning off on the town road beyond.

Carrick let the second hand of his watch tick off a full minute before he got out of the Humber and walked across to the *Karmona*. Aboard her, the two men who remained broke off their discussion as he reached the trawler's iron-plated deck, the service technician obviously glad of the distraction but the trawler engineer balefully unfriendly at the sight of the approaching Fishery Protection uniform.

'Looking for someone, Mister?'

Carrick nodded. 'Peter Blayett – is he still around?'

'No.' The trawlerman grunted his monosyllabic answer.

'Just missed him, chum,' said the technician more cheerfully. 'He's gone up town for a spell, and I can't say I blame him. If I was skipper of this load of trouble, I'd get away from it too.'

'So the skipper's just left,' said Carrick casually. Twice now, it seemed, he'd caught out Peter Blayett – and left himself with a question growing in importance. For what reason were Helen Elgin and Shona Bruce involved in this punctured deception? 'Expect him back soon?'

'Don't know.' The *Karmona*'s engineer eyed him suspiciously. 'Why?'

'Business with him.' The trawler's deck gear might be old, but it was well maintained. Grease hung in fat globules from the winch pawls, the trawl warps and cordage were neatly stowed and in good condition.

'There's no rush – I can come back.' He put his hands in his pockets, a man apparently in no hurry. 'Didn't expect him back in so soon, that's all. More engine trouble?'

'Fuel-pump failure,' volunteered the technician. 'Almost the ruddy same as before. Och, I've had more damned trouble wi' this one job than wi' any other all year.'

'Don't blame us,' grumbled the *Karmona*'s engineer. 'Think we like limping back like a ruddy lame duck?' He sniffed and wiped an overalled arm across his nose, transferring more grease to his face. 'Let's get on with it.

Or d'you want us to stay tied up here till blasted doomsday?'

'I'm ready, mate.' The fuel technician grimaced apologetically towards Carrick and disappeared down the engine-room ladder. The trawlerman gave another sniff, then followed. Left alone, Carrick shoved his cap back from his forehead, looked around, and saw a solitary deck hand up for'ard, sheltering under a tarpaulin while he wielded a paintbrush along a row of red, football-sized net floats. The deck hand returned his gaze with lazy hostility, lit a cigarette, and went on painting.

Carrick quit the trawler, returned across the drizzle-soaked quay, and climbed back aboard the Humber. After a moment's thought, he started the car and drove round to the harbourmaster's office.

Bill Duart, the duty harbourmaster, had his desk by a window overlooking the harbour breakwater. He raised a surprised eyebrow when he saw his visitor.

'Thought *Marlin* was sailing about now, Webb. Don't tell me you've jumped ship to get away from old Shannon?' He enjoyed the thought.

'Any day now, Bill.' Carrick liked Duart, an ex-Navyman whose reasons for being ashore were tied up with drawing a war disability pension and having a metal hook where his left hand had once been. 'Like to do me a favour?'

'This is Tuesday, and I don't get paid until Friday,' warned Duart. 'Money apart, name it.'

'Keep an eye open for one of the local line-boats, the *Rachel C.*,' said Carrick. 'I want to know when she comes in. Tell the rest of your boys, will you?'

'Easy enough.' Duart scribbled the name on his pad. 'Where do I reach you?'

'I'll check by phone,' said Carrick. 'What do you know about the *Karmona*, Bill?'

'Our favourite trawler?' Duart scratched his head with the tip of the hook. 'The skipper's a tall character called Blayett, an' this is the first time she's been up this way. She's been in an' out of here for a couple of months –

85

mostly in. But as long as he pays his harbour dues, the rest is his worry.' His curiosity was roused. 'Why the interest, Webb?'

'Routine stuff.'

'And I should mind my own business?' The harbourmaster sat back. 'Well, they landed two good catches after they arrived. But, since then, I doubt if they've managed to get their trawl damp, let alone catch anything in it. An engine'll only last so long, and that one must be overdue at the scrapyard.' He broke off and jerked his head towards the window. 'There goes *Marlin*. Could be a rough patrol, this one.'

The fishery cruiser was in a hurry. Blue Ensign flapping fitfully at her stern, she bucked and heaved as she breasted the growing swell at the harbour's mouth. Then she plunged on, steering southwest and building up speed, heading out to where the heavy clouds were beginning to give way to brighter sky.

'Weather reports still the same?' asked Carrick.

'The same. This rain won't last, and I'll bet on sunshine within the hour. But the storm's still building up, according to the forecasters. Really building. When it comes –' he glanced down at his hook – 'well, now and again I feel almost happy about having a shore job.'

'How long till it breaks?'

'Maybe tonight, maybe tomorrow.' The harbourmaster was philosophical. 'All depends on an Atlantic depression, a big 'un – the thing's just wandering about, as erratic as a clockwork mouse.'

Carrick nodded. 'October's the month for them. Bill, have you a corner of a shed or an office we could use to stow some gear?'

Duart considered for a moment, opened his desk drawer, and produced a key. 'There's a little place over on the north quay. Not much more than a watchman's hut, but it's empty. That do?'

'Fine.' Carrick took the key. 'Mind if I use your phone?'

'Help yourself. But keep it brief, will you?' Duart pushed the instrument across.

86

He checked the directory, then dialled Helen Elgin's home. She answered almost before the ringing tone had got under way.

'I heard you were back,' she told him. 'Shona called me from the reactor station . . .'

'She told you about the suit?'

'Yes.' The line carried only its background hum for a moment. 'Webb, what does it mean? The police have been here too – Chief Inspector Deacon says the funeral can't go ahead.'

'It means a lot of people are having to change their minds,' said Carrick quietly. 'Helen, can you pinpoint the place where your father disappeared?'

'Fairly closely, yes. Why?'

'I want to go out there, using your father's boat. I need a guide.'

He heard her draw a sharp breath. 'You're going under?'

'Yes. I want to make sure one thing is there – and learn more about something else.' He didn't elaborate.

'I'll come. Give me half an hour, and I'll meet you at the harbour.' She hung up.

The arrangement meshed sweetly, even the weather. Moments after Clapper Bell reached the rendezvous, officially cleared by the Crosslodge unit, a taxi drew up at the quayside and deposited Helen Elgin. She wore a fawn waterproof jacket over corduroy slacks and a maroon jersey, and the taxi driver handed Carrick a heavy leather grip which she'd brought along.

'I'm going under with you,' she told him. 'Mind if I don't give my reasons – not yet, anyway?'

'I never say "no" to unpaid help.' He grinned at her, hefted the grip down into the launch, where Clapper Bell already had the engine ticking over, then helped her aboard before he cast off the mooring line.

From the harbour, the launch curved out and round the high bulk of the headland hills towards Culzean Bay. Iron-grey and threatening at first, the sea around them changed to a deeper translucent blue-green as the last wisps of laden, dark, rain clouds disappeared above and the sun shone down. An occasional wave, larger than its fellows, still broke over the launch's bow and drenched them with spray, but for the most part the swell had moderated and the launch, hugging close to the coast, was a good sea boat. Carrick left its running to Clapper Bell, and spent most of the time giving Helen a quick summary of the morning. Only one thing he avoided, his knowledge of Peter Blayett's connection with the *Karmona*.

The time for that would come.

The petrol-engine's note slowed as *Marlin*'s bo'sun throttled back a notch and turned the little craft's nose into the sweep of the bay, not far from the futuristic bulk of the nuclear station.

'Like to give me the marks, Miss?'

'The pillar rock over there is one.' She ran the tip of her tongue over her lips, tasting the dried salt spray. 'Line it up with the Crosslodge sphere, and have us more or less parallel with that clump of trees near the headland.'

'Fine,' said Clapper Bell approvingly. The launch engine bellowed again, and a quartet of mallard, bobbing amid the wave crests, took to the air in hasty fright.

'Webb –' She half-turned on the thwart, her manner worried. 'I'm being as accurate as possible, but . . .'

'It's never easy,' Carrick agreed. 'But if we get a rough approximation, it should do.' It was a problem the landsman seldom pondered. Once visit a place ashore, and all but the most casual observer could return to the exact location. But the sea wasn't so considerate, its surface held few signposts.

At last, Helen Elgin was satisfied. They dropped a mooring grapnel over the side, cut the engine, and, as the boat swayed gently to the swell, the two men set to work unpacking the aqualung equipment.

'You won't need diving rubbers.' Her voice made them turn. She had stepped out of the slacks, and now pulled the sweater over her head to expose the rest of the form-

88

fitting, one-piece bathing suit underneath. 'The water's different here.'

Carrick dipped one hand over the side. She was right, the sea was perceptibly warmer – Stark's description of 'a giant teakettle' came back to his mind.

'Saves time,' he agreed, stripping down to his own swimming trunks. 'Clapper, you stay with the boat for now.'

The fair-haired giant acknowledged the order, ran a quick connoisseur's eye over the girl's trim figure, then helped them into the aqualung harnesses.

'All set?' Carrick made his own check – rubber-sealed wrist compass, depth gauge, flippers comfortably firm, weight belt secure, the cork-handled double-edged knife – one edge heavily serrated – in its leg sheath. He spat on the glass of his face mask, rubbed it over, then gave the result a quick rinse in sea water. The chemical industry still had to come up with a demisting solution to match human saliva in effectiveness – he watched approvingly as the girl did likewise then pulled her mask into position. 'Let's go then.'

She went in first, stepping backwards over the stern, floating gently until he joined her. He pointed downwards, she nodded, and they duck-dived down, finning towards the bottom, legs moving in a smooth, regular crawl beat.

A familiar numbing, and Carrick cleared his ears. Then, the demand regulator valve clicking steadily, a thin trail of exhaled air bubbles pluming from his outlet tube, he continued on. The water darkened as they descended, but the Scottish west coast seas have a clarity few others can match, and every detail of the rock and weed was clear below. Fish darted from their path, mostly codling and an occasional haddock, circling as curiosity overcame initial alarm.

At six fathoms, they reached bottom, sinking down and disturbing a low, slow-settling cloud of sediment. A moment's pause, and Carrick pointed to the girl, signalling to the left. She held up a thumb in acknowledgement and slowly, swimming close to the rock, using the launch's mooring rope as the centre of their radius, they began their search.

She swam well, arms by her side, fins moving steadily, a style which conserved both air and energy. He came closer, let himself reach out for her hand, and felt her fingers twine lightly in his own. Her face mask turned towards him, their eyes met, and then they kept on, air bubbles feathering together.

Young, broken rock and time-smoothed shingle, low waving shrubberies of red-green wrack and darker kelp, the floor of the bay was the home of a proliferation of minute silver fish and scuttling crabs, creeping sea snails and poised, patient barnacles, threadlike scarlet worms and blue-shelled mussels. It was a place where a myriad variety of life forms dwelled in a pulsating kill-and-be-killed, eat-and-be-eaten rhythm of rudimentary existence – but Carrick also knew it as something more. It held beauty, beauty which coruscated to lure, blended pastel in protection.

The girl knew it too. She pulled at his hand, gestured him over, and they sank down again beside the close-spiked, multicoloured shapes of a clustered colony of sea urchins, a miniature forest of guarding quills.

Carrick looked, nodded, and then signalled they should go on. But, after another ten minutes of fruitless searching, he decided on a break and pointed upwards.

They rose together through the brightening water, broke surface near the boat, and were helped back aboard by Clapper Bell.

'Any luck, sir?' Air tanks on his back, he was eager to go.

Carrick removed his mouthpiece and pulled off the face mask. 'We drew a blank, Clapper. Have a try further out, to the south.'

'This could be m'lucky day.' The bo'sun quickly eased his bulk over the side, adjusted his mouthpiece in the water, and sank downwards. Carrick watched for a moment as his companion's shape was quickly distorted by the shifting, deepening lens of water, his trail of air bubbles moving steadily away from the boat. When he turned again, Helen Elgin had removed her weight belt and air cylinders and was towelling her hair.

'Glad you did it?'

'Very glad.' She lowered the towel and stretched her long, slim legs. 'I said I wanted to, Webb. But until I went down, I didn't know if I'd be able to face it again – not here, not after what happened.' She smiled ruefully. 'Still, we didn't have much luck from your point of view, did we?'

'We haven't finished.' Carrick glanced back at the water, disliking the task ahead. 'Helen, there's another reason I asked you here. What's the truth about Peter Blayett? Why call a trawler skipper an insurance agent?'

She flushed, carefully spreading the towel into a neat oblong on her lap while droplets of sea water ran down her suit to the firm white flesh of her thighs.

'That was a pretty stupid thing to do,' she admitted slowly. 'But Shona – well, I did it because Shona asked me. It's a separate thing, Webb. Nothing to do with this.'

He said nothing, just watching her, one arm resting on top of the engine-hatch cover.

'Shona's family are line-boat fishers. Her father has given it up, retired. Her uncle, well, you've met him, you know what he's like. They used to own half a dozen boats, operating out of Kintyre, but the trawlers wiped them out in the old days when there weren't the same restrictions. The Bruces hate trawlermen of any kind. Shona was terrified her uncle would find out about Peter. That's all there is to it.'

'You mean –' Carrick found it hard to believe, yet impossible to deny the ring of truth in her voice. 'You mean that because of her family, and nothing else –'

She finished it for him. 'Shona and I always go around together. So we decided that I'd say Peter was – well, my property. The insurance-agent pose was his own idea, and we steered clear of every chance of his meeting Shona's people.'

'Did anyone in your own circle know he was a trawlerman?'

'My father did.' Her mouth twisted wistfully. 'He thought it was quite a joke. But he kept it to himself. There's nothing else we've hidden from you, Webb. Look, I'm meeting Shona and Peter this evening. Will you come too, come and hear it from them?' She gave a sudden shiver. The wind was springing up again, coming cold-edged from the northwest.

'I'll be there.' He moved towards her, took her jacket, and placed it over her shoulders. Then, slowly, deliberately, he pulled her towards him. The kiss began gently, exploring at first then harder, her lips suddenly as demanding as his own, her hands gripping his shoulders, the soft curves of the swim suit pressing against his chest, the wet material warm from her body.

Just as suddenly, she wriggled free and flopped back against the engine bulkhead. 'I'd like a cigarette.'

He had lit one for each of them when they heard a noisy splashing in the water near the bow. Clapper Bell's head of spiky fair hair had broken surface, and he was waving an L-shaped length of metal in one hand.

'You reckoned this position pretty well, Miss,' said the burly seaman triumphantly once he'd been helped aboard. 'Found it lyin' on bare rock, less than forty yards south o' here.'

'Anything else in sight?' demanded Carrick.

Bell shook his head. 'That was the lot.'

'Helen?' Carrick held the crank handle towards her.

She looked at it and nodded. 'It's ours, definitely. When it was new, there was a rubber grip on the handle. Look, you can still see what's left of the rubber down at the collar.'

Carrick laid the handle on the launch's centre thwart. By itself, it wasn't evidence. If there had been fingerprints, the sea would have long since removed them . . . as it would have removed other traces. But combined with the sliver of glass, it gave him his own mental picture of what had happened to the elderly marine biologist. The attack in his boat by another frogman, the brief struggle, the crank handle grabbed, the stranger's face plate smashed, then, perhaps, a second man, the end of the struggle and Elgin overpowered – it had all been the prelude to death.

He looked at the sky once more. Fresh grey clouds were building, and the wind was roughening the sea. 'Time we were making back to harbour.'

They dried off and changed, Carrick and Clapper Bell at the bow, the girl at the stern, haste a greater virtue than modesty.

Fastening his trouser belt, *Marlin*'s bo'sun winked. 'You had me real worried for a bit, Mr Carrick,' he murmured.

'Why?' Carrick fastened the last buttons of his shirt and reached for his jacket.

Bell chuckled. 'I foun' the crank handle pretty quick – bit o' luck, nothin' else. But when I came back up wi' it, you were busy wenchin'. So I goes back down for a bit, not wantin' to interrupt, like. But you get tired sittin' on your backside on a rock ten fathoms down . . . sir.'

Chapter Five

Rolling, white-capped waves and sudden heavy squalls of rain battered the launch on the last half mile of its return journey, and they were glad when the harbour appeared ahead. Other craft were heading in – fishing boats, large and small, crews who had decided their safety margin was near to an end. The quayside berths were filling up.

There was, however, still no sign of the *Rachel C*. She could be on her way or, more likely, Joe Bruce had decided to take her into some other, nearer shelter.

Once the launch was tied up, they went ashore and stowed the aqualung gear in the harbour office's store shed. That done, Clapper Bell drifted off for a liquid lunch, prelude to another gossiping prowl around the harbour area.

'Helen?' Carrick raised a questioning eyebrow.

'If that's an invitation, the answer's yes,' she agreed. 'But I can't take too long. I've an appointment with a lawyer this afternoon – he's handling my father's estate.'

They settled for a restaurant meal in the town's High Street. When the girl had gone, Carrick lingered over another cigarette before paying the bill and walking down the rain-battered street and across to County Police Headquarters. The Ayrshire force inhabited a large grey stone-fronted building in Charlotte Street, close to Ayr Fort – the latter an historic old ruin which had been a church almost before there was a town, then a fortress, and finally, ingloriously, a cavalry stable.

Chief Inspector Deacon's office was on the first floor. A small, cluttered room, it had a gas fire burning in one corner, the windows were steamed and an anaemic potted geranium hung limp from an ironwork basket on the wall opposite his desk.

'Come in, come in.' Deacon swooped from behind his desk, radiating welcome as he took Carrick's rain-soaked coat, placed it on a wire hanger, and hung it on a nail behind the door. Carrick left his uniform cap on an empty space on top of a filing cabinet, and found himself waved towards a chair.

'Like a cuppa?' Deacon's hand hovered over the desk buzzer.

'No – I've just eaten.' Carrick found the change from the policeman's previous cynical toleration difficult to accept.

Deacon seemed to read his thoughts. 'I'll say it for you,' he volunteered. 'I was wrong, and I'm admitting it. Carrick, I like to think of myself as a good cop – and when I make a mistake, then I work like hell on squaring my personal ledger.' He tapped the desk. 'That's the nearest to an apology I've made in a long time. What's next on the agenda?'

'Something we found out under the bay.' Carrick told him of the crank handle.

'Interesting – like that splinter of glass your boss Dobie passed on to us. Our forensic boys say it's identical in optical quality and gauge to a skin-diver's face-mask glass.' He hunched forward in the chair. 'I've done two things, Carrick. One of my constables is a member of our local skin-diving club. I've got him working on a list of all members and any known unattached divers living in the area. On top of that, we're contacting every scuba stockist within fifty miles, checking on all purchases of face masks within the last fortnight.'

'What about Elgin's house?'

'Fingerprinting, you mean?' Deacon wasn't hopeful. 'We can do, but it's an overrated pastime. Even the dimmest of the population have come round to wearing gloves when they go breaking and entering. It would be a lot

95

more useful if somebody could tell us what Elgin was working on.'

'His notes have gone.' The policeman's random choice of phrase sparked an idea in Carrick's mind. 'But maybe there is a way – a back-door approach. Elgin left plenty of specimen jars lying about. If we turned another marine biologist loose on them, he might come up with an idea.'

It was worth a try. He used Deacon's telephone to call Fishery Research headquarters in Edinburgh, made the arrangements, then rose to go.

'Any help you need, just let me know.' Deacon said it earnestly, as no mere good-neighbour gesture.

'Then here's a starter,' Carrick told him, pulling on his coat. 'Run a check on a Peter Blayett. He's skipper of the *Karmona*, one of the trawlers in harbour. I'd like his background – anything you can get.'

'What's the angle?'

'Nothing definite yet.' Carrick opened the door and gave the policeman a whimsical grin. 'But that may change after tonight.'

From the police station he walked down towards the harbour, stopped at a telephone box to check the address of the local branch of Orbis Fuel Sales and Service, then collected the department car from the port parking area, and set out.

The Orbis branch was a quarter hour away, sited within the fringe perimeter of Prestwick International Airport. Carrick located their building, tucked away behind a succession of maintenance hangars and airline installations, spent a few moments talking his way past the barricade lines of outer office and private secretary, and was finally shown into the Orbis manager's room.

'Fishery Protection?' The manager, a briskly efficient Canadian, eyed the uniform with interest. 'It isn't often we have your outfit visiting us. Aircraft are our main business.'

'But you're servicing a trawler in harbour at the moment – the *Karmona*,' said Carrick. Somewhere out on the main runway an airliner's jets whined to vibrant life.

'Don't remind me,' said the Orbis manager ruefully. 'That's why you're here?' As Carrick nodded, the Canadian lifted the internal telephone on his desk, and dialled a number. 'This won't take a moment.' He gave a brief grunt of satisfaction as his call was answered. 'Maintenance? Is Archie Sanderson back yet?' Hand over the telephone mouthpiece, he explained, 'Sanderson's been handling the *Karmona*.' Then he turned his attention back to the instrument. 'He's there? Good – send him along, will you?'

Carrick waited until he'd hung up. 'Just what's wrong with the *Karmona*'s engine?'

'That's what we'd like to know.' The jet outside began its takeoff run, and the Canadian sat back until the thunder of its engines had passed them. 'Marine work is pretty much a sideline with us – a useful one, but still a sideline. We supply diesel fuel and there's a contract-rate maintenance service. We make money on the fuel, and as long as the maintenance side breaks even, we're happy. But this one –' He gave a mock shudder, then looked up as there was a brief double-knock on the door. 'Come in.' The door opened and the Orbis technician Carrick had last seen at the harbour entered the room. 'Archie, this is Chief Officer Carrick. He wants to talk about your trawler.'

'Not mine, please.' The Orbis technician gave a smile of recognition. 'I want nothing to do with it, believe me.'

'You know each other?' The Orbis manager was curious.

'We met on the *Karmona*, this morning,' explained Carrick. 'Sanderson, you said fuel-pump trouble then. You're sure?'

'Seems to be.' Sanderson shrugged. 'Och, I don't know what the heck's going on. The first time it broke down, I gave the pump a straightforward service. They went out for about a week, then in they came, shoutin' for help again. So I fitted a new pump – first day out, it seized up. It's never ended since – I've spent the morning fittin' the third ruddy replacement pump this month. Either the engineer they've got is a ruddy incompetent, or I'm losin' my grip.'

'But she's worn out, isn't she?' probed Carrick. 'Couldn't it be just general old age?'

'Old?' The technician shook his head. 'The hull maybe, but there's nothing wrong with the engine. It's almost brand new, and bigger than most of her size!'

'Supposing someone was deliberately interfering with the fuel pump, would that account for what's been happening?' Carrick saw the other man frown.

'You mean sabotage or somethin' –'

'Just interfering.'

'Well – yes, it could. But –'

Carrick stood up. 'That's all I wanted to ask. Is the job finished?'

The manager nodded. 'It's finished. But what you're suggesting, Chief Officer . . .'

'Is officially off the record,' Carrick told him. 'It's vital it doesn't get back to the *Karmona*.'

The two men agreed, and he was satisfied.

By five o'clock, Carrick was driving out of town again. The rain had stopped, dusk was falling, and a strong, gusting wind blew ripples of wet, fallen leaves from trees and hedgerows. His destination, Glenconnel Hotel, a new sprawl of glass and concrete, was set five miles beyond the Ayr boundary and had been created strictly for the carriage trade. A neon glow in the distance marked its location, and to reach it from the main road he turned off and drove along a twisting private avenue. At its end, the hotel parking area was already two-thirds filled. Other traffic was coming in as he left the department car and crossed to the building.

Inside, the Glenconnel was busy as usual. Carrick crossed through the foyer, ignoring the array of tourist-bait showcases filled with Scottish tartans and mock-antique silver, checked his coat, and made his way to the Clan Bar in the west wing of the hotel.

Blayett and the two girls already had a table near one of the windows, with a vacant chair awaiting him.

'The order to date is two gin and Italians and a cognac,' announced the trawler skipper. 'Like to complete it?'

'Whisky, straight,' Carrick told the waitress, a plump twenty-year-old in a tight, perspiration-stained black dress and a tartan shoulder sash. She nodded wearily and left them.

'Well, Carrick, do I draw an official reprimand – or are you going to arrest my ship? Not that the ruddy thing looks like going anywhere!' Blayett maintained the same air of amused embarrassment as he glanced at the dark-haired girl by his side. 'You know, Shona, it just wasn't very clever. Right now I've got a crew who wants to know why the Fishery Patrol are taking such a sudden interest in me. I've also an uncomfortable intuition that you and I probably rate low on a local popularity poll.'

Shona Bruce was repentant yet defiant. 'I'm sorry, Webb. But just supposing I'd said, "Meet Peter, who is supposed to be an insurance man, but isn't, just as he's supposed to be dating Helen but isn't –"'

'You can see how it was,' said Blayett. See it my way, man to man, added the look which went with it. You know what women are like, a pure amalgam of ideas and notions. The only sensible policy is to either humour them or get out fast – and right now I'm humouring.

'No harm done,' Carrick told them, and turned his attention towards Helen, whose plain cocktail sheath of dark-blue wool was set off by a single strand of matched pearls. 'This afternoon go all right?'

She nodded. 'Just papers to sign – and more police waiting when I got home. They were looking for fingerprints.'

Chief Inspector Deacon, at least, didn't seem to be wasting time.

The waitress returned with their drinks and talk halted for a moment while Blayett paid with a handful of change.

'What do we drink to?' asked Shona Bruce, lifting her glass.

'Luck,' suggested Blayett. 'Just luck all round.'

Carrick sipped his glass. 'It's in short supply right now.'

'I should know,' said Blayett ruefully.

'What happened this time?' Helen asked.

'Fuel pump – the same old fuel pump,' said the trawler

skipper viciously. 'We're outside the Firth at midnight, off the Mull of Kintyre, with the echo sounder graphing fish all around us and the trawl ready to be lowered – then it acts up again. A few coughs and splutters, then we're floating around with a dead engine, the sea building up, and a storm warning on the radio. We had to work like blazes to rig up a temporary repair.'

Carrick took a longer sip at his drink. The Mull of Kintyre was roughly fifty miles to the west, across open water to the opposite side of the Firth. Provided the *Karmona* had been outside the restricted area, it was Blayett's business where he chose to fish, just as it was his business if he chose to come back to Ayr on an allegedly faulty fuel pump – if it was really faulty.

'You took a bit of a chance coming back here,' he commented. 'I'd have ducked into Campbeltown as the nearest port.'

'A chance?' Blayett's face hardened for a moment, then just as quickly he resumed his old, easy confidence. 'Well, we came anyway, hobbling home.' He gave a wink. 'This place has its attractions, Carrick. Anyway, the servicing agents are here.'

Shona Bruce had her head on the trawlerman's shoulder. 'How long till you sail again, Peter?'

'Tomorrow or the next day.' Blayett gave a brief grin. 'But this time the pump better be right. If it isn't, I've told the local service rep exactly what I'm going to do with it.' He swallowed the last of his drink. 'Time for another round, then let's eat.'

'My round.' Carrick signalled the same plump-built waitress, circling the glasses with his forefinger. She gave a sigh which threatened to split her dress seams and was back in a couple of minutes, the four fresh glasses on her tray. Carrick paid, then pushed back his chair.

'Must make a phone call,' he told the others. 'I'll be right back.' He left them, went out to the hotel foyer, located the public call box, and dialled the harbourmaster's office at Ayr.

'Chief Officer Carrick?' The duty man at the other end of

the line greeted his voice with relief. 'We've got one of your men here. Hold on.' The line was quiet for a moment, then Clapper Bell's gruff tones echoed in his ear.

'You still lookin' for the *Rachel C.*, sir?'

'She's back in?' Carrick glanced at his watch. It was not quite six-thirty.

'No, and she won't be,' said Petty Officer Bell laconically. 'Remember tellin' me that old Dobie was bringin' down *Snapper* from the north, sir?'

'What about it?' Carrick was as much anxious as impatient. *Snapper*, the smallest of the fishery squadron ships, was due in the Clyde area by now. It would be ironic if the new arrival had started off her patrol by stopping and boarding the one boat with which he was so vitally concerned.

'*Snapper* spotted wreckage late this afternoon off the West Kintyre coast,' said *Marlin*'s bo'sun dourly. 'Picked up three bodies and identified the boat.'

'The *Rachel C.*?' Carrick swore softly and bitterly.

'Aye. They're bringin' the bodies back to Ayr. *Snapper* radioed she'll be in port in about another hour.' Petty Officer Bell waited for a response. 'Sir? You still there?'

'I'm still here, Clapper,' said Carrick grimly. 'All right, I'll come right back.'

He put down the receiver, stared at himself for a moment in the phone-booth mirror, then went out to tell Shona Bruce.

'You don't have much chance wearing seaboots and oil-skins.'

Three dead men, lying side by side on the deck in one of *Snapper*'s tiny cabins, each man covered in a blanket, underlined the truth of the statement. Captain MacVey, the fishery cruiser's commander, looked at the bodies with a detached compassion, then shrugged towards Carrick. 'Ever ask yourself how many seafarers can swim, Webb? Damn few, that's the answer. The whole thing's wrong, shouldn't be allowed.'

Carrick had heard it before. The subject was Jock Mac-Vey's perpetual hobbyhorse. 'Where'd you find them?'

'Machrihanish Bay. Well, to be accurate, that's where the wreckage was spotted by a coaster. We were passing by, going for the Mull of Kintyre, when we picked up his signal. We went back, found the bodies, then collected a lifebelt and a few spars of wood.' MacVey shook his head. 'Poor devils must have been on their way back in with a good catch, judging by the amount of dead fish floating around. Know much about them, Webb?'

'Not as much as I wanted,' said Carrick. Jock MacVey was exactly a year his senior in both age and Fishery Protection service, and they knew each other well. That apart, *Snapper* had received the signal which had gone out to the fishery squadron, detaching Carrick for unspecified duties. 'The big fellow with red hair is named Joe Bruce, and I've got his niece in a car on the quayside. Bruce sailed with two of a crew yesterday afternoon, making darned sure nobody knew just where he'd be fishing.'

'They're like that, plenty of them,' agreed MacVey. 'Well, it's part of the business. Why broadcast the fact you've found a good fishing mark? But it looks as if this storm caught them on the hop – and they may not be the only ones.'

Snapper had arrived in harbour at 1915 hours, coming out of a gale of howling wind and wild, foaming seas which were still pounding in unremitted fury against the outer breakwater. The news had spread, and a small crowd of dockers and fishermen had watched silently on the quayside as she'd made fast to her berth. Carrick had been among them, having left the two girls with Blayett in the latter's car, and once *Snapper* was secured he'd been first to board her. She was a neat little craft, though less than half the size and power of *Marlin*. Her design was perfect for her usual station, patrolling the shoaling inshore waters of the northwest or the equally treacherous rocks and shallows of the Hebridean chain.

'Give me a hand, Jock.' Carrick bent beside the first body, removed the blanket, and began to search the pockets.

'Do we have to do this? I mean – if they can be identified –' *Snapper*'s captain seemed doubtful about the decency of the procedure. 'The civil police should be here soon.'

'It won't take long.' Carrick continued his self-imposed task. The first two members of the crew of the ill-fated *Rachel C.*, men he'd never seen before, had only ordinary, everyday items in their pockets. One, a small man with a grey beard, had a religious medal on a chain around his neck. The other, young, the characteristic foam of death by drowning still oozing from his mouth and nostrils, had a picture of a girl glued inside a gun-metal cigarette case.

Joe Bruce's body he left until last. A small hip flask and a heavy clasp knife, a bundle of pound notes which were now so much sodden paper in one hip pocket – Carrick gave a grunt of interest, as he located a thin, well-worn leather wallet in the man's inside jacket pocket. Receipts, bills for fuel oil, and a couple of betting slips, he set aside. But one scrap of paper was more interesting, though the ink had run and become blotched from its immersion. Carrick had seen the handwriting once before, when he'd checked through Dr Elgin's work book.

'Can you make it out, Jock?' He passed the wet slip of paper to *Snapper*'s captain, gathered the other items together, then, on second thoughts, put the wallet into his own pocket instead of returning it. 'I'll give you a receipt for the wallet.'

'Huh? Fine – do that.' MacVey peered at the paper in the dim light of the cabin. 'What's this phrase here? I've got most of the rest . . .'

'Let's see.' Carrick joined him. '"Not to go against", Jock.'

They read it over between them. Undated, stiffly, rather formally phrased, it was more of a memo than a letter.

Sunday evening.

Dear Joe,

Though your boat will not be required immediately, I will need at least one further charter trip as before, probably in two weeks time. While I will advise you the exact date as soon as I can, meantime please keep that period clear if possible. I must emphasize that the situation must remain confidential, and in the interim I know I can rely on you not to go against my advice.

Ernest Elgin.

'What situation?' asked MacVey.

'A lot of people would like to know that, Jock,' said Carrick softly. 'Look, how was the weather out there?'

'Where we found them?' *Snapper's* captain wrinkled his brow. 'Rough enough. They were probably caught in a sudden squall – there's plenty of broken patches to this storm, high and low.'

'A sturdy boat and an experienced crew, just like that?' Carrick clicked finger and thumb together.

'It's happened before now.' Jock MacVey was wary without really knowing why. 'What's biting you, Webb? There's the father and mother of a gale blowing, and accidents happen.'

'They happen all right.' Carrick folded the paper carefully and put it in his inside pocket. 'Mind if I see the wreckage you picked up?'

The debris from the *Rachel C.* was under a tarpaulin on *Snapper's* afterdeck. While Clapper Bell held a heavy battery lamp, Carrick checked it over – a wooden grating, the single life jacket with RACHEL C. stencilled on the back, some fish boxes, a half-empty oil drum, and a hatch cover, constituted the meagre collection. He replaced the tarpaulin and went back to the fishery cruiser's bridge.

'Jock, where are *Marlin* and *Skua* located?'

MacVey puffed his cheeks in thought. '*Marlin* was riding out the weather off Campbeltown Loch when I heard from her last. *Skua's* down in the North Channel, probably tucked in shelter by now.'

'Then *Marlin*'s nearest to the spot.' Carrick lit a cigarette on his own. Jock MacVey's taste was restricted to thin black cheroots, smoked only after meals. 'Jock, will you radio her for me? Tell Captain Shannon to –' He grinned, thinking of Shannon's fiery temperament. 'Suggest to him that the moment conditions improve he should get out there and collect any other debris he can find.'

'He'll want to know why,' warned MacVey.

'Then we'll tell him,' said Carrick. 'Tell him that I don't believe in coincidences, especially when nobody hears a distress call from the boat and it goes down so ruddy quickly that not one of three men have time to put on a life jacket. Jock, there was a trawler near that area last night, a trawler I'm interested in, with a skipper who says he had engine trouble. The odds are the engine trouble was faked – and broadcasting the fact he was off Kintyre could add up to a smoothly planned piece of double bluff.'

Snapper's captain looked at him steadily for a moment, then gave a low whistle. 'You really mean it, don't you! Webb, if even a suggestion gets out that there was something odd about this sinking there's going to be hell to pay. We'll have a war on our hands, with every fishing port on the coast as a battleground!'

'Then we keep quiet about it until we're sure. You'll send the message?'

'I'll code it now – and keep hoping you're wrong.' MacVey strode off towards the radio room.

Clapper Bell was gossiping with his opposite number on *Snapper*'s crew when Carrick found him near the gangway. He broke off the conversation and came smartly across.

'Finished, sir?'

'Finished here. Clapper, what's the word the *Karmona*'s crew are putting out about her breakdown last night?'

His companion sniffed. 'That the engine failed off the Mull of Kintyre and they practically paddled her back. I was drinkin' wi' a couple o' them this afternoon. Out of uniform, like – the uniform puts a lot o' the lads off.'

'Friendly?'

'Friendly enough if you're buyin' – but they don't talk

much. A pretty miserable bunch, an' some of them know damned little about the trawlin' game. A deadbeat crew for a deadbeat boat.'

'Don't be too sure of that,' warned Carrick. 'The *Karmona*'s not such a tub as she looks. Clapper, I want her underside checked. Can you do it? Tonight?'

'The water's pretty black inside harbour.' Petty Officer Bell glanced speculatively along the quayside to where the trawler was berthed. 'Depends what I'm lookin' for, sir.'

'Any trace of damage. The kind of damage a steel bow might take if it ran down a light wooden hull.'

'Like the *Rachel C.*?' Clapper Bell took the implied suggestion impassively. 'I can have a look, sir – but these old-timers are sturdy. She could go through a line-boat like a knife through butter and carry hardly a trace.'

'Try it, but don't take chances,' Carrick told him. 'We've got enough trouble without canvassing for more.'

Marlin's bo'sun gave a quick grin. 'It's a bit busy roun' about here. I'll leave it for a spell, then work out o' the other side o' the harbour – the aqualung gear's over there in the store shed anyway.'

'I'll be back in a couple of hours,' said Carrick. 'I'll meet you at the shed.'

He left Bell gazing out at the harbour scene, studying and memorizing the surface layout. From *Snapper*, he walked along the quayside to where he'd left Blayett and the two girls. The red M.G. was empty, but a thin, sea-booted trawlerhand, a cigarette dangling from his mouth, was standing near it.

'Your name Carrick, Mister?'

'Yes.'

The man slouched nearer. 'The skipper's taken them over to the *Karmona* – he tol' me to bring you along.'

'Fair enough.' Carrick followed the man the rest of the distance to the trawler. Clapper Bell soon going underneath her hull, himself being invited aboard – the incongruity of the situation was appealing.

His escort guided him straight to a cabin set just below the trawler's wheelhouse. Blayett opened the door to the deck hand's knock, then dismissed the man with a curt nod.

'Come on in, Carrick,' he invited. 'I thought it would be better for them to wait here.'

Carrick entered. The skipper's quarters on the *Karmona* were small, fitted only with the bare essentials, but tidy. Helen Elgin and Shona Bruce were sitting side by side on the narrow bunk, and the smell of stale cigarette smoke added to the trawler's other workaday odours.

Shona Bruce looked up at him. 'You've – you've seen my uncle?'

'Yes.'

She looked away again, her hands plucking nervously at her skirt. 'Will I have to see him?'

'No, not unless you want,' he told her.

'I don't think so.' The dark-haired girl was visibly relieved. 'We were never very close. Webb, how did it happen?'

He shrugged. 'Hard to say. A storm squall, a freak wave – these things just happen.' He turned towards Blayett. 'What would you say?'

'Conditions were bad enough where we were,' said Blayett easily. 'Where'd they find the wreckage?'

'Machrihanish Bay.'

'Then we were fifteen, twenty miles to the south,' mused Blayett. 'Far enough to make a difference.'

Helen Elgin had been sitting quietly. Now she stirred, got up from the bunk, and stared out of the cabin's single porthole into the darkness beyond. 'Why should it happen?' she asked bitterly. 'Webb, was there anything –'

'I looked. Just a note in his wallet, from your father. Dr Elgin wanted to charter the *Rachel C.* for another trip, but no details, no date. You knew they'd been out before?'

'It happened every now and again,' she said. 'The last time was about a month ago – they were gone for a couple of days. It's standard marine biological practice to go out like that, cruising and sampling –'

'For plankton?' Blayett lounged back against the cabin door. 'He told me about it once. What's the connection anyway, Carrick? I know you thought Joe Bruce might have been able to help you with some answers about Helen's father, but how?'

'I wouldn't have been sure myself till I'd talked to him,' said Carrick grimly. 'Well, that chance has gone. But there are always relatives who might know something. Shona, what do you think?'

'Dr Elgin and Uncle Joe went out alone on these trips,' said the girl dully. 'They could handle the *Rachel C.* between them. But you could try my father – he might have heard something about it.'

Carrick glanced at his watch. 'How about going now?'

'All right.' She hesitated. 'Will he know . . .'

'About the sinking? The police will have told him.'

Blayett pursed his lips. 'Mind if I don't come? Sorry, Shona – it's not the old family feud that's bothering me. I've got problems to sort out, plenty of them, before we sail. Suppose I telephone you later tonight, and we can fix a date for tomorrow?'

He went with them from the cabin to the quayside, then headed back towards the trawler.

It was a twenty-minute drive from Ayr along the coast road to Troon, where Shona Bruce's father lived in a small rented house close enough to the shore for the upstairs bedroom windows to give a view of the sea. A tall man in his late sixties, but bent and moving slowly and painfully, his hands swollen with the rheumatism of too many years of damp, wet living conditions, Matthew Bruce gave his daughter a formal, on the surface unemotional welcome which had a private warmth of its own. He nodded gravely towards Helen Elgin, then shook hands with Carrick as they were introduced.

'The police were here earlier,' he said in matter-of-fact fashion. 'Well, live by the sea and it makes its own claim.' He looked down at his hands, then cleared his throat. 'You two lassies could make a cup o' tea for us if you like.'

They took the hint and went off. Matthew Bruce led

108

Carrick through to the front room, where a bright fire burned in the hearth.

'The police told me a Fishery Protection ship found the bodies,' he said. 'Is that why you're here, Mr Carrick?'

Carrick shook his head. 'No. It's a bad time to come asking, but I'm here for information about something else.'

'Aye.' The older man sat down, picked up an empty tobacco pipe from the table and sucked it thoughtfully. 'About Joe and Dr Elgin?'

'Yes.' Carrick was surprised, and showed it.

'Which makes you the second who's been here tonight for that reason,' said the fisherman shortly.

'Who else? Did you know him?'

'Aye. Mr Hinton, the reactor manager up at the power station. He was here just after six o'clock.' The pipe left his mouth and he spat unerringly into the blazing fire. 'Then two hours later the police are at the door, telling me about Joe.'

'You know Hinton by sight?'

'It was him. Shona took me out to Crosslodge a while back, when they were givin' guided tours for visitors – a guest day they called it. I met him then.' He grunted, and eased himself into a more comfortable position. 'An' whatever it's about, all I c'n tell you is what I told him. Joe could be close-mouthed when he wanted. All he said about that last charter trip was that he'd caught a fair kittle o' fish while the doctor was busy wi' his wee sample nets and bottles. I don't know where, and I didn't ask.' He sucked the pipe again, his face softening in the firelight's glow. 'There were four o' us, Mr Carrick, four brothers, wi' Joe the youngest and me the oldest, all at the fishing from when we left school. Joe's the third to be claimed out there. Just me now – me and Shona.'

'Even so, perhaps this time you've been lucky,' said Carrick gently.

'Lucky?' The old fisherman's crippled hands made their own mute, angry protest.

'Lucky tonight. Lucky that you didn't know the right answer.' Carrick glanced round as the door opened and

Shona Bruce came in, carrying a tea tray with cups and saucers. Helen Elgin was behind her, also laden. 'Shona, did you or Helen ever tell Alex Hinton that Helen's father sometimes used the *Rachel C.*?'

They stopped where they were. Shona Bruce bit her lip, then nodded. 'I think I did, once – but that was after Helen's father disappeared. We were talking about what had happened, and I think I told him then.'

'Helen, go back to the evening when your father vanished. Could Hinton have known that your working late would mean your father going out alone?'

She frowned. 'Perhaps. I just don't know.'

But Carrick's mind was made up. 'Where does he live?'

'Hinton? At Corriebreck – it's a cottage just beyond the power station,' she told him, her voice puzzled. 'But Webb, won't he be working late at Crosslodge, completing the check Mr Stark ordered?'

'I don't think so. Mr Bruce, have you a telephone?'

The fisherman shook his head.

'I'll find one.' Carrick stopped at the door. 'Shona, your father will tell you what this is about. Can you and Helen make your own way back to Ayr?'

'By bus, yes.' The tall, raven-haired girl was equally nonplussed. 'But where will you be?'

'Calling on Hinton.'

There was a telephone box at the end of the road, and Carrick used it to make a call to Chief Inspector Deacon. But the policeman was out, down at the harbour according to the tired-voiced C.I.D. duty man who took the call.

'Any message for him, sir?'

'Tell him I'm going to Alex Hinton's home,' said Carrick. 'Say I think Hinton's involved – he'll understand.'

He replaced the receiver, went back to the department car, and began driving. It was one of the few times he'd pressed the big Humber to the limit, and it responded magnificently, surging through the gears as it took the succession of corners on the winding, narrow road which led south. Further along, he took the left-hand fork which joined the broad straight of the brand new motorway by-pass beyond, dodging Ayr with its narrow streets and clogging traffic. He gave the big six-cylinder engine's three litres of power their head, and the motorway's width became a dark, rushing tunnel, pierced by the car's glaring headlights.

Carrick thought as he drove. Hinton – well, why not the Crosslodge reactor manager? Hinton had visited Matthew Bruce before official word had reached shore that the *Rachel C.* had been sunk. But if Hinton had known from another source, and had then had a job to do? Accept that the *Rachel C.* had been sunk to silence Joe Bruce, and it could have been Hinton's task to check, to make sure that no one remained who possessed that same fragment of information. It had been a clumsy move, but someone's hand might have been forced, forced by the same circum-stances which had ruled that the *Rachel C.* must not return.

He took the Humber in a vicious four-wheel drift round the banked roundabout at the motorway's midway point, steadied the wheel by sheer wrist strength and tyre adhe-sion, and pressed on, ignoring the angry horn blare from a slow-moving petrol tanker. Now another fact glared at him, was still nagging in his mind as he reached the end of the motorway stretch and allowed the car to slow down for the narrower road beyond.

If Hinton had been forced to come out into the open, it must mean things were also about to come into the open at Crosslodge – and that what mattered most now was happening beyond the nuclear station's boundaries.

Corriebreck Cottage sat close to the main Ayr–Culzean road, an isolated, single-storey building with a large, ram-bling garden fringed by trees. Carrick nearly overshot it – the car's headlamps swept over the building as he took a sharp turn in the road, and he braked just short of the postbox which marked the start of the cottage's gravel path. He pulled the car into the grass verge, switched off lights and engine, and got out.

The front of Hinton's home was in darkness, the only sounds the rustling trees, the wind whining on the road-side telephone wires, the faint spit and crackle of the Humber's cooling exhaust pipe. Carrick's feet crunched on the first stretch of the gravelled path and he left it quickly, walking across the grass at its side. As he came nearer the cottage, his angle of view changing, he saw a glow coming from the rear of the building. A moment later, skirting round the humped shape of a garden roller, he saw the source of the light – the back door of the cottage lay open.

The same escaping glow glinted on the polished paint-work of a small black Volkswagen saloon standing without lights in the open, to one side of an old potting shed. He crossed towards it and looked in. A suitcase lay on the back seat. He felt the slow warmth still rising from the little car's rear engine, gauged that it had been stopped for a good few minutes, and set off cautiously towards the house.

The cottage kitchen was bright lit, modern in its fittings, and empty of life. The door beyond was open, and gave him a view of the short, darkened hallway beyond. Two doors led off it to the left, and another to the right – and a crack of light showed under the first door on the left.

A board creaked underfoot as he crossed the threshold. There was an immediate scurry of movement from some-where within, the crack of light disappeared, and there was silence once more. Someone else was in the cottage, someone who knew he had arrived, someone in no hurry to find out the who or why.

'Hinton?' Carrick called, then waited, listening. The squeal of wood on wood reached his ears, and he darted across the kitchen to the hallway beyond, throwing open the door on the left. He had a glimpse of drawn curtains and a shadowy figure already halfway over the low win-dowsill – the same moment he began a dive for the floor as the figure's right arm moved in a fast, pointing arc.

Two shots and their echoes blended almost into one,

muzzle flames stabbing. The first bullet smacked into the plaster wall behind him, the second buzzed past his ear and whined in ricochet off something more substantial. Carrick rolled over fast, knocked over a low table and, as it crashed on its side, a third shot whined past his shoulder. The figure vanished from the window, he heard feet running on the gravelled path outside, then a car door opened and slammed shut.

He reached the window as the Volkswagen engine screamed to life. Still without lights, the car lunged forward, spinning wheels throwing gravel as its driver clawed for acceleration. Carrick was through the opened window and running as the Volkswagen, driver hunched behind the steering wheel, took the corner of the house wide, its nearside tyres running on grass. A snarl of torn metal and a spangling of glass rang out as the car's nearside wing brushed the garden roller, but the Volkswagen kept on until it reached the foot of the pathway. Then it stopped, two more shots blasted out, the car's lights blinked on, and it was accelerating again, travelling south along the main road.

Carrick sprinted down to the road, reached the parked Humber then stopped, defeated. One of his front tyres was bullet-punctured, flat and useless. He turned, walked back to the house, located the telephone in the hallway, and called County Police Headquarters.

This time, there was a distinct change in the manner of the C.I.D. duty officer once Carrick identified himself and even before he had sketched what had happened.

'Chief Inspector Deacon's already on his way,' the man said tersely. 'You got the number of the car, sir?'

'No.' Carrick swore again, this time at his own imbecility.

'Not to worry. We'll find it.' The man hung up.

Carrick replaced his own receiver, then switched on the rest of the cottage lights. The room at the back seemed to have been a combination of lounge and library. Desk drawers lay open, and the ricocheting impact of the second bullet was explained by the deep dent in a heavy metal storage heater. He went through and checked the other rooms. One was a bedroom, a disarray of opened drawers and scattered clothing; the other, a small dining room, was neat and orderly. It amounted to the classic picture of a man poised to run.

There was a torch in the kitchen, and he took it and went out to the potting shed. The door swung open with the wind when he turned the handle, and the searching torch beam lit on a variety of paint and oil cans, tools, a small workbench and a battery charger. Hinton seemed a keener handyman than gardener, mused Carrick, finding a light switch and clicking it on. He went over to an old wooden chest in one corner, lifted the sack draped across its top, then froze for a moment, staring down at the contents. Aqualung cylinders, rubber suit, fins, and weight belt – a complete skin-diving outfit was stored neatly below. He found the face mask, sniffed the still-new odour of the rubber, and was still staring at it when headlights swept up the pathway to the cottage.

Two cars braked to a halt near the shed. From the first came Chief Inspector Deacon and two of his men. The doors of the second car opened a moment later, and John Stark, the Crosslodge production director, came out followed by Dunn and two more policemen, shielding their eyes as they moved across the glare of the headlamps.

'Been having trouble with friend Hinton, eh?' Deacon's face hardened as he saw the face mask in Carrick's hands. 'I've ordered roadblocks, and there's a "special search" message going out on the west-area radio net. We'll nail him.'

'I should have got that car number,' said Carrick angrily.

'Aye, it was a mistake. But I've made at least one myself tonight.' Deacon jerked his head towards the two Crosslodge men. 'They'll tell you why. You've been biting your nails over what this was all about, Carrick. Well, we know now, and it's big, damned big.' He broke off for a moment, ordering two of his men to stand guard at the foot of the pathway.

114

'What's big?' Carrick grabbed the policeman by the arm. 'Look, Deacon, when somebody starts shooting at me I want to know why.'

'Uranium, that's why,' said Deacon grimly. 'Our little reactor manager seems to have removed enough of the stuff to build a power station of his own.'

Uranium – Carrick felt his mind freeze at the word.

'Aye, I thought that would quieten you,' said Deacon philosophically. 'And don't ask me what it's worth. The nearest to sense I can get out of Stark is that this makes a mail-train robbery look like amateur night at the church hall.'

'When did you find out?'

'About ten minutes ago. I was down at the harbour, routine stuff about the *Rachel C.* sinking, when I got a message from Stark saying he had to see me at Crosslodge right away.' He grimaced. 'That's how the lines got crossed. I was starting out for Crosslodge when your message came in over the radio – and I thought it must mean you were heading there too. Panic, confusion – either way, it was my fault.' He gestured towards the cottage. 'What's it like inside?'

'Three bullet holes, some half-emptied drawers, and an opened window,' said Carrick briefly. 'There was a suitcase in the car.'

'It's a wise man who knows when it's time to leave, and Hinton is no fool.' Deacon nodded. 'Well, I'll take a look around – and I'll want the bullets out of your car tyre too. Mind if my lads take off the wheel, and put the spare on for you?'

'Saves me a job,' agreed Carrick. 'What about Stark and Dunn?'

'Let them cool off for a wee moment,' growled the county man. 'What brought you here anyway?'

'The *Rachel C.* Hinton went to see Shona Bruce's father this evening, before anyone knew about the sinking. He was pumping to find if the old fellow knew where Dr Elgin went on his last survey trip.'

'Before?' Deacon whistled. 'That sounds –'

115

'Sounds as if he knew the *Rachel C.* wouldn't be coming back,' agreed Carrick. 'Elgin and three fishermen – four deaths so far.'

'And you came damned close to being number five.' Deacon cocked his head to one side. 'Any ideas about the boat?'

'Nothing tangible – yet.' Carrick took a cigarette from the policeman's offered pack, and accepted a light. 'Not until we find some more of the wreckage.'

'Hmm. Well, it's by the way, but I've had a rundown on your trawler skipper.'

'Blayett?' Carrick drew the smoke deep into his lungs. 'Well?'

'Aged thirty-five, native of Hull, the family black sheep – but only in a minor way.' Deacon shrugged. 'Seems he grew up among fishing boats, then went Merchant Navy, deep sea. He was charged with smuggling once – that made it easier for us, finding he had a C.R.O. file.'

'Much in the smuggling charge?'

'No. Happened two or three years after the war. He was just a kid helping to run cigarettes and nylons across the Med – anyone who had a boat was in on it then. Socially acceptable sport. The French threw him in clink for a year, and when he got out he went off to Malaya to grow rubber or something like that. Seems he came home about a year ago, picked up the *Karmona* at scrap value, rounded up a crew, and has been doing all right since – except when the old tub breaks down. Satisfied?'

'As far as it goes.' Carrick sensed the need to speak and judge on fact, not suspicion. 'Just that he features on the fringe of a whole list of loose ends. The *Karmona* was out at the same time as the *Rachel C.*'

'And so were a whole lot of other boats,' said Deacon pointedly.

'He also happens to be making a considerable play for Shona Bruce.'

'Stark's secretary?' Deacon allowed himself the luxury of a chuckle. 'From what I've seen of her, that's no crime. Still, I could put a tail on him when he's ashore.'

116

'If you watch him outside the harbour, I'll take care of the rest,' agreed Carrick. 'Right now, all I want is to hear from Stark and Dunn.'

'I'll get them in – I've a couple of jobs to pass on to my lads anyway.' Deacon walked across to the waiting group. He returned in a moment, followed by the two power-station men. They went into the cottage kitchen, Stark's hands clenched deep in the pockets of his overcoat, Dave Dunn more grey-faced than ever.

'Well now!' Deacon picked up a tin of fruit from the kitchen table, glanced at the label, then stood juggling it from one hand to the other. 'Let's have a quick run through this again, Mr Stark – for my own benefit as well as Carrick's.'

'But what about Hinton?' Stark drew himself indignantly erect, his small eyes balefully angry behind their spectacle lenses. 'Don't you realize what's involved?'

'The machinery's in motion,' soothed Deacon. 'I'm better here, waiting for something positive, than away dashing up and down half a hundred country roads with nothing to go on but wild hope.'

Stark seemed to simmer down a little. 'Start with Dunn, then,' he told them. 'It began with him.' He nodded to his chief engineer. 'Go on man, tell them.'

'Well –' Dunn swallowed and moistened his lips. 'You were there this morning, Mr Carrick, when Hinton and I were told to make a complete check of the station?'

'And I gave you the contact list.' Carrick nodded.

'Yes – they were all clear, the contacts I mean. That is, except for the mortuary attendant – he handled the rubber suit, and –'

'Never mind the damned suit,' snarled Stark. 'Get on with the rest.'

'Sorry.' Dunn shuffled his feet. 'Well, we'd covered more than two thirds of the station area and found everything in order up till then. But about – oh, five-thirty it must have been – Hinton came to me and said he'd have to go out.'

'You'd been working separately?' asked Carrick.

117

'No. Together. But the office staff leave just after five, and we'd stopped for a few minutes to make sure there was nothing urgent on our desks –'

'Urgent?' Stark sniffed, then fell silent as Carrick glared at him.

'What reason did he give for leaving?'

'An – an urgent telephone message that was waiting.'

'Which didn't exist,' said Deacon conversationally. 'At least, not according to his secretary. But he has a private line which bypasses her – and the station switchboard.'

'He just told me about the message,' protested Dunn. 'I said I'd carry on till he got back. Only he didn't come – and then, when I found the shortage, I – I contacted Mr Stark.'

'Time?' asked Carrick.

'Minute or two after eight,' grunted Stark, taking over the story. 'I was still in my office, holding on for their final report. I heard Dunn out, checked that Hinton passed out of the main gate at five-forty and hadn't been back, then called the police.' He spotted a spider running across the linoleum floor and ground it viciously underfoot. 'Don't ask me how, but we've a shortage of approximately seven hundred uranium cartridges – seven hundred of them!'

'How big is each cartridge?' Carrick glanced at Deacon and saw that the policeman too was struggling to grasp the full significance of the theft.

'Mostly a foot long. Some of them larger.' Stark's small mouth tightened. 'But they're U238 cartridges, and they've been burned in the pile!' He saw the blank expressions on their faces and gestured impatiently towards his chief engineer. 'You tell them, Dunn. Make it simple – simple enough for them to understand!'

Dunn nodded. 'The bulk of uranium is U238 – we give the name because its atoms each have 92 protons and 146 neutrons. But a tiny number of atoms are different, fissile, with only 143 neutrons – U235. You follow?'

'More or less,' said Deacon cautiously.

'Good. We use roughly three thousand uranium cartridges in one – ah – stoking of the reactor.' Dunn was at ease now, speaking of a world he could both understand and command. 'The main blanket is natural U238, but there is a small central core of enriched U235. U235 can go critical. Assemble a critical mass without precautions, and . . .' He spread his hands in bland illustration. 'Of course, basic station procedure at Crosslodge makes this impossible. And the main blanket is ordinary, non-enriched.'

'But why steal this "ordinary" uranium after it has been used?' demanded Carrick. 'It's finished. Or – is it?'

Dunn shook his head. 'A piece of uranium not much bigger than a sugar cube could drive a train completely round the world, Mr Carrick. It could meet the power needs of a town like Ayr for months. What would be left afterwards – the waste, you might call it – is not like the ash left after a coal fire has burned out. With uranium, something new is created.

'When a nuclear reactor goes critical, when it is producing power, the U235 irradiates the blanket mass of U238.' He sensed their struggle to comprehend. 'Gentlemen, I'll spell it out. We produce a lot of heat. At the same time, the one kind of uranium changes the other. U238 becomes another substance called neptunium. Neptunium is unstable. It promptly changes itself into another man-made element – plutonium.'

'You mean the atom-bomb stuff?' Deacon very gently laid the fruit can back on the table.

'The atom-bomb stuff,' said Dunn softly, his dislike of the subject plain on his face. 'Plutonium is element 94, the high explosive of nuclear science. Certain chemical treatments would have to be carried out to extract it from the irradiated fuel rods. But the plutonium-based atom bomb is the – the detonator – of the hydrogen bomb. What is missing from Crosslodge, gentlemen, is enough raw material for several of these detonators.'

Chapter Six

No nation that possesses the secret has yet released a textbook guide to the construction of the nuclear bomb. But the principle is horrifying in its simplicity, and it is the refinement of control that is so thankfully complex. There is one further safeguard that places the nuclear weapon beyond the reach of many a covetous outsider – the need for a basic supply of man-created plutonium.

'Basically, all that is needed is to assemble enough fissile material in segments which are harmless when kept apart but which become super-critical the moment they make contact,' said David Dunn. 'It would be rough and ready, but effective.' He gave a mild cough and pointed a bony forefinger out the cottage door towards the potting shed, where two of the county detectives had begun rummaging. 'I'd rather they didn't do that, Chief Inspector. At least, not until we've run a Geiger counter over this place.'

Chief Inspector Deacon swallowed, nodded, and galloped off to halt the activity.

'If I thought you meant that literally –' Carrick mustered a grin as he read the wisp of hitherto unsuspected humour in the Crosslodge engineer's eyes.

'There's not a situation where a potential atom bomb is lying around in jigsaw pieces,' agreed Dunn, as unconcernedly as another man might discuss the price of garden fertilizer. 'But the fuel cartridges do constitute a radiation hazard.'

'And getting the plutonium out of them?'

'Means a complex chemical process.' John Stark spoke, his voice still bitter with anger. 'All used cartridges are returned to the Atomic Energy Authority for the extraction. We play no part in it, beyond taking special precautions before they're sent off by rail.'

'Special precautions.' Carrick found the phrase ironic. 'Then how could this size of a shortage remain hidden?'

'Sheer, flagrant duplicity!' Stark banged his fist on the kitchen table. It was theatrical, but effective. 'Every nuclear-power station carries a certain uranium reserve. Our reserve stock has one figure in theory, another in fact. The number of used cartridges withdrawn from the reactor and the number actually returned appear to balance – until someone takes all three sets of figures and counts off the actual material in storage. Then the whole thing dissolves into a paper fiction.'

The type of trick any cashier might use to cover up a second-rate embezzlement – Carrick could understand both the simplicity and the short-term effectiveness of the method.

'And getting the stuff out of Crosslodge? How many people in the station would have to be involved?'

'In the deception?' Stark quivered. 'Just one, a man in executive authority like Hinton. Don't ask me how he moved them. For all I know, the situation's so – so fantastic that he may have ordered the staff to load them on trucks!'

Dunn was more moderate in his assessment. 'It could have been done piecemeal, by one man, provided he knew the appropriate precautions. As long as you know what you're doing, there's no difficulty about handling radio-active materials.'

'Huh.' Chief Inspector Deacon trudged back into the cottage. 'Well, I've stopped the men from nosing around, and I've checked with headquarters. So far, there's no sign of the Volkswagen.' He pursed his lips, thinking of the night of work ahead of him. 'Talking about how the stuff was moved?'

'One logical answer is by sea,' said Carrick softly. 'By sea . . . and Dr Elgin's bad luck was finding out about it.'

'That's presumption, pure presumption.' Stark flushed. 'Well, maybe not completely. We've finished the analysis tests on Elgin's equipment. He'd been in contact with a radiation source which could have been the uranium – the Health Unit can't be positive. But there's a constant security watch on our shore perimeter, Carrick. It's just as thorough as on the landward side. A boat couldn't just sail in and load the stuff aboard. The only vessels allowed to come in are Atomic Energy Authority craft, all with hand-picked crews, sailing direct between here and the Authority port in southern England. Suspecting them would be like – like suspecting the Royal Navy of operating piracy as a sideline!'

Deacon fidgeted. The county policeman was mournfully aware of one thing – that an inevitable deluge of security men, government departments, and worse, was about to break over his head. 'Maybe we should talk more about this back at Crosslodge,' he suggested. 'And, eh – you think you could get somebody out to check this place for radiation, Mr Stark?'

'Right.' Stark pulled his coat tighter across his shoulders. 'Though don't imagine you're going to find the cartridges buried in his garden.'

'Aye, that's too simple to hope for.' Deacon sighed unhappily. 'You coming along, Carrick?'

'Yes, but only to borrow an item.' He glanced towards Dunn. 'Could you fix me up with a Geiger counter, a lightweight job?'

'Easy enough,' Dunn agreed.

'Fine.' Carrick decided to partly satisfy their curiosity. 'Seems to me it'll be a handy thing to have around – particularly while Hinton's on the loose.'

At Crosslodge, Carrick stopped only long enough to collect the Geiger counter, a slim tube little bigger than a fountain pen and fitted with a pen-type pocket clip. He signed a receipt – more than ever, Crosslodge had become red-tape conscious – then drove away.

Minutes after ten p.m. he steered the department car

into the harbour area at Ayr, turned towards the north quay, and stopped close to the metal-framed store shed.

The harbour scene was quiet, and the wind had dropped. Beyond the breakwater, waves still boomed and shot their spray skywards, but the storm was quietening, and, at least for the moment, its fury was passing. Carrick left the car, walked across to the shed and found the door unlocked, with only one of the two sets of aqualungs still lying within. He went out again, and stood by the edge of the dark quayside, looking across to the other side of the harbour, where the dark silhouettes of the vessels in port showed against the glow of the town lights beyond. Stark lines of masts and funnels, occasional pinpoints of cabin lights, the nearer slap and chuckle of water against a moored cabin cruiser all blended to form a poetry of their own.

The tide was coming in, bringing swirling motion to the harbour's floating flotsam of driftwood and oil slicks. He heard a splash as a rat left an under-pier staging, then it appeared below him, swimming in a rippling vee of arrow-straight progress. The water swirled again, but the rat fought free of the current and returned to course, bound on some mysterious errand of its own. He felt a grudging admiration for the rodent's determination, but another swirl on the harbour surface brought different results.

The rat splashed in a hurried dive, to reappear a distance away, swimming in a fresh direction, its action now swift and panicking.

At the same moment, Carrick began tearing off his jacket and shoes. The new swirl in the water was round a black shape which floated listlessly, a limp, face-down figure with the twin air tanks of an aqualung strapped to its back!

The cold dark water hit him like a shockwave as he dived into it from the quayside, and he closed towards Clapper Bell's helpless form in a pounding overarm-crawl stroke. Carrick reached the man, turned him on his back in the water, saw the closed eyes beneath the glass face plate, pulled the aqualung mouthpiece from between the loosened jaws, and began towing him back towards the quay.

It took every ounce of strength he possessed to drag *Marlin*'s bo'sun from the water on to a low concrete staging, and he didn't waste time attempting to haul him up the steps to quayside level.

First he freed the face mask, unzipped the front of the rubber suit, and felt the faint pulse of life at Bell's throat. He spent a few precious seconds dragging the man still further clear of the lapping water, and then – water-soaked clothes adhering to him like a cold, flapping second skin – he dashed up the steps and across the quayside to the store shed.

He came back with the small emergency cylinder of oxygen which was part of their standard diving gear, pulled his heavily built companion over on his left side, cracked the cylinder valve, and held its hissing cup-shaped mask over Bell's mouth and nose.

What followed was a time for waiting.

First, the pulse grew stronger; next, the chest perceptibly began to rise and fall. After three minutes, Clapper Bell gave a groan. At four, he stirred and his breathing strengthened. Carrick fed him the oxygen for a few minutes longer, then closed the valve and let nature take over.

Bell's eyes opened slowly, recollected fear was etched in the lines of his face as he tried to take in his surroundings. He moved his head, saw Carrick, and forced a grin.

'You look pretty wet, sir.'

'And you look worse,' said Carrick thankfully. 'You also owe a vote of thanks to a harbour rat.'

'Eh?' Clapper Bell raised himself into a half-sitting position, winced, and shut his eyes. 'I've one hell of a headache – och, that was a damned stupid thing to let happen.' He took a deep, lung-ballooning breath, then another. 'Carbon dioxide build-up – me! The kind o' thing you expect a beginner to dodge, an' it happens to me!'

Carrick helped him out of the aqualung harness. 'Did you reach the *Karmona*?'

'Aye.' He took another deep breath. 'You got a fag handy, sir?'

'Hold on.' Carrick retrieved his jacket from the quayside above and returned with the cigarettes. He lit one, gave it to Bell, then lit another for himself, shivering.

'Thanks.' The fair-haired giant gave a shaky grin. 'Well, I got out to the *Karmona* all right – came up once on the way, then stayed under. Checked her bow to stern like you wanted – more feelin' wi' my hands than anythin' else, the water was so black. That's probably why I didn't catch on at first my eyes were startin' to go. Next thing I'm seein' double, my head starts poundin', and I'm pantin' like a greyhound. "Watch it, boy," I told mysel' an' flushed the mask with extra air –'

Carrick nodded. 'Better late than never.' It was the standard remedy for a carbon dioxide build-up, caused by shallow breathing not bringing in enough fresh air from the tanks.

'But it didn't work,' said Bell, his confidence still shaken. 'I'd left it too late. I'm tryin' to get as far away from the *Karmona* as I can, an' then I know I'm goin' to pass out. I dumped my weight belt – but after that, the next thing I know, I'm lyin' here, wonderin' who the hell's standing over me.' He grimaced. 'Made a proper muck of it, didn't I?'

'That's about the strength of it.' Carrick jerked his thumb. 'Come on, up on your feet. You know the drill – start moving.'

Bell groaned, but obeyed. Carrick helped support him up the stone steps and across the quayside to the shed.

'Keep walking around and moving your arms. Get as much air into your lungs as you can. I'll be back.' Inside the shed, he changed into his own diving rubbers, strapped the second aqualung harness into position, slipped the borrowed Geiger counter into the suit's inner pocket, and was ready.

'You're goin' over?' Bell broke off his exercise routine when he came out. 'I'm pretty certain there's nothin', sir.'

'This is different,' said Carrick shortly. 'Something new

has turned up.' He walked down the stone steps, adjusted his face mask, and went into the water. A fathom down, he began finning. After a minute, he resurfaced briefly to check his direction, blinked, and automatically rubbed a hand across the facepiece to clear his water-blurred vision. But the blur remained – and his breathing was quickening.

He sank down again, flushing his lungs with extra air from the tanks. His head began throbbing . . .

A scant thirty feet from the *Karmona*'s side, Carrick deliberately surfaced, removed the aqualung mouthpiece, and floated for a moment, breathing the pure night air. He was near enough the trawler to hear the rumble of voices coming from the crew quarters for'ard, then laughter. A man appeared on deck, coming from the fo'c'sle, glancing around, then disappeared down the engineroom companionway.

Carrick blessed his luck for the second time. After another moment, his head still throbbing, he began a slow, surface breast stroke back across the harbour. His arms and legs felt like lead and the distance seemed interminable – but at last he was there, and Clapper Bell was helping him on to the concrete staging.

'You all right, sir?'

'In – in a minute.' Carrick sat down on the bottom step, knew his legs were shaking, fought until they steadied, then gestured the puzzled, waiting seaman back to the shed. He said nothing until they were under its roof.

'Got a match, Clapper?' He rough-dried his hands before he took the offered box. 'Turn on my air supply. Just a little, a trickle.' As his companion obeyed, Carrick struck a match, let the flame get a firm grip on the wood, then held it close to the aqualung mouthpiece.

The flame went out, not guttering as in a wind, but dying as he watched. He struck another match, then another. As each flame reached the mouthpiece area, its life ended. He repeated the experiment with the other aqualung set, with the same result.

'Clapper, I owe you an apology.'

Bell scratched his head. 'I don't get it – what's wrong wi' them?'

'You've just seen a demonstration of how to commit murder.' The words came like coarse-ground ice. 'When were these cylinders filled?'

'Aboard *Marlin*, but I topped them up this afternoon, m'self, sir. Found a garage wi' a compressor that could do the job.'

'Then brought them back here, and locked them in the shed?'

'Aye, that's how it was.'

Carrick walked over to the door. It boasted a medium-weight padlock, but he concentrated his attention on the exposed hasp plate, held by four screws to the wood of the door. 'Wouldn't take long to loosen these, Clapper, and bypass the padlock.'

'No –' Clapper Bell's mouth opened, then closed hard. 'You mean some lousy . . .'

'Came in and fixed both lungs, Clapper. Probably bled off air from each, topped the pressure up again with a cylinder of carbon dioxide, and left us to do the rest. If one of us had dived and hadn't come back, then the other would have gone down to help –'

'And we'd both have stood a ruddy good chance of never comin' up,' concluded the petty officer. 'Is that what happened to Dr Elgin?'

'With minor variations, yes.' Only a rat's frightened panic had prevented it happening again and two more bodies, air-exhausted, all the post-mortem symptoms of accidental death by CO_2 poisoning present, being finally found on the beach or against some harbour wall.

'Maybe I was right, then,' growled Bell.

'About what?'

'That time I came up near the *Karmona* – I'd a feelin' there was somebody standin' there on deck, seein' me but doin' nothing,' said Bell in a hard, quiet fury. 'The murderin' baskets! But how did they know we'd dumped our gear here? The harbourmaster wouldn't broadcast it. Think they maybe followed me?'

'There's only one other way,' said Carrick. He'd solved one mystery, but had presented himself with another problem he liked even less. 'There was somebody with us when we opened the shed, Clapper.'

'The girl?' Bell shook his head in disbelief. 'Not that one, sir. Not the Elgin girl. Hell, she's on our side, isn't she?' He blinked. 'Well, isn't she?'

Carrick could only shrug – and hope that his instincts were true.

They changed, Carrick locating a dry pair of khaki-drill slacks and a shirt in his duffel bag, and topping them with his uniform jacket. That done, both still shaky and exhausted, they loaded the aqualung gear into the department station wagon.

'Nothing more tonight,' decided Carrick. 'We find a hotel and get some sleep.'

'Suits me, sir,' agreed Bell. 'But what about the *Karmona*?'

'Still too many theories, too few facts, Clapper. Anyway, neither of us is fit enough to even try to get out there again right now.'

Petty Officer Bell didn't attempt to argue. They drove from the harbour, out along the seafront, and booked in at the Sandercombe, a large, holiday-trade hotel with the temporary advantage of being almost empty in the October off season. They cleaned up, left their gear in their rooms, and Carrick arranged with the night porter to have his water-soaked uniform slacks dried and cleaned by morning. Then the two met for a drink in the downstairs lounge.

Bell buried his nose in a tankard of draught beer and was content to leave it like that. Carrick nursed a whisky and sketched out what had happened at Crosslodge.

'The newspapers'll have a real ball wi' this story,' declared Bell surfacing from the tankard's depths as Carrick finished.

'You won't find a line of it in print,' Carrick told him. 'There's a thing called a D notice – D for Defence Regulations. Editors get them every now and again. Proprietors get something different, a quiet word of advice. Even if there's the odd firebrand editor prepared to go to jail for a story, there's not a board of directors in the country who'd swop port and pheasant for bread and water.'

'Aye. Sort o' like ten days in an open boat and no mess steward –' Clapper Bell chuckled at the hoary piece of sea-going cynicism, then shook his head. 'But who'd buy this plutonium stuff?'

'You want a list?' Carrick took another drink from his glass, and let the mellow warmth of the whisky trickle through him. 'At least a dozen nations – the little fellows who're already throwing their weight around. Right now they're a long way behind the starting gate in the nuclear game, and both sides of the Iron Curtain have sense enough to want to keep 'em that way. Look, Clapper, these characters are selling an end product their customer couldn't duplicate. Once they've got it, they're more than halfway towards developing the finished article. It would be pretty ramshackle, and they wouldn't be in full membership of the nuclear club – but people don't get in your road when you can mention you've a couple of atom bombs handy in the locker.' He yawned, and drained his glass. 'I'll call the police and let them know where we are. Afterwards, I'm going to bed. They start serving breakfast at eight a.m. – I'll see you there.'

He woke early the next morning, and was glad of it. Sleep had drifted into a nightmare in which Crosslodge and the *Karmona* blended and reblended while he struggled deep down in a sea which was thick, black, and overpowermg. Through it all, floated a procession of figures, figures without body or substance, yet with the faces and voices of Blayett and Helen, Hinton and Shona Bruce, even Stark and the final horror of a man whose face was a pulsating blank and whose hair grew in scattered, disconnected tufts. Once he came out of sleep, sweating, the sheet gripped tight between his fingers . . . his mind told him that carbon dioxide was the trigger for the hallucinations, but the pillow became an enemy, grey dawn a welcome friend.

When he went down, Clapper Bell was already having breakfast, carving his way through a plate of crisp fried bacon and smoked haddock, with all the impartiality of a steam shovel. Carrick settled for scrambled egg, toast and coffee, took the morning paper his companion had discarded, and flicked through the news pages. Not as much as a line was in print to indicate the slightest thing amiss in the county.

'Nothin' like a decent spot of grub first thing.' Bell mopped up the last remnants on his plate, emptied his coffee cup, and sat back with a sigh of contentment. 'Well, what's the programme, sir?'

Carrick glanced at his watch. It was eight-thirty, and the world should be coming to life. 'Here's a start. Get the aqualungs recharged, then go down to the harbourmaster's office and see if Bill Duart can give you a list of all shipping movements in and out of Ayr over the last month.'

'The lot, sir?' Clapper Bell raised an expressive eyebrow. 'It'll take time.'

'The lot. Tell him it's vital, and tell him I'll be looking in for it before noon.' The steel-hooked harbourmaster was going to love him for this, but, without the list, one move he was shaping would be impossible to implement.

'Fair enough.' The burly seaman pushed back his chair. 'Anything else, sir?'

'That'll keep you going for a spell. But meet me with the Humber outside Dr Elgin's house in an hour's time.'

Bell nodded and went off. Carrick finished breakfast, had a cigarette while he caught up with the newspaper's comic section, then headed for the nearest telephone and called Chief Inspector Deacon's office.

The county policeman's voice was tired and edgy when he answered his extension. He appeared to brighten a little when he recognized his caller, but sank back almost immediately into the same dulled gloom.

'We found Hinton's car this morning.' His voice crackled over the line. 'Abandoned in a lane just off the main Ayr to Glasgow road. Looks like it was lying there most of the night. The suitcase was gone. Nothing else left worth bothering about.'

It was logical enough. Hide in lonely countryside, and a new arrival sticks out like a sore thumb. But Glasgow offered a chance to submerge among more than a million other human ants, and Glasgow was also a seaport which offered a chance to escape abroad, provided you had both money and contacts.

'Any further forward at Crosslodge?'

'Them!' Deacon made it sound worse than an oath. 'No. Man, I don't know where you've been all night, but any sleep I've had has been at this desk – you've been well out of it, believe me. Now there's a pack of Atomic Energy Authority security men in ruddy residence – flown them up overnight from London. Special Branch have moved in from Glasgow, and there are others to come. I'm being used like a blasted office boy, Stark's getting edgier by the moment, and Dunn looks like he's expecting the end of the earth. But they were right about one thing. Nothing, but nothing, has used the Crosslodge jetty apart from Authority vessels sailing to and from Authority ports. Their crews are security screened so damned tightly it's a ruddy wonder anyone below the rank of admiral gets a job.'

'I can tell you how Dr Elgin was killed,' said Carrick as the tirade ended. He told Deacon of his own experience.

'Aye, a diabolic idea, but interesting,' mused the policeman. 'These lads play it clever – and rough. Still think it was your trawler pals?'

'Or a friend of theirs,' said Carrick evasively. 'I'm going to have another try at checking the *Karmona* during today. You're still watching Blayett?'

'For what it's worth,' grumbled Deacon. 'He hasn't stepped outside the harbour since last night . . . and I need all the men I can get.'

'Keep it going for a little longer,' pleaded Carrick. 'If I'm right –'

'And if I'm wrong –' Deacon sighed again. 'Och, I'll do what I can. Any time you want me, I'll be here – for the next ruddy month or so, by the look of things.' He hung up.

Carrick replaced his own receiver. A little later he left the seafront hotel. The tide was out, exposing a long expanse of almost deserted sandy beach, high-water mark outlined by a thick banking of dark green seaweed and other flotsam cast in by the storm. But in contrast with the previous night there was next to no wind, the sea was millpond calm, and a faint haze of mist was beginning to gather off shore, curtaining off the horizon, swallowing up the black specks which were motor drifters and other fishing boats once more heading out of harbour.

It should be a good day – for most people.

He walked the half-mile distance to Helen Elgin's house, to discover both girls not only up and breakfasted, but with a visitor in residence.

'An early start to the day.' Professor MacEwan extended a thin, bony hand. His grip was cold and limp, but his manner friendly. 'Your doing, I believe, Chief Officer – you asked Fishery Research to examine Dr Elgin's specimens, and, well, I decided you might as well have the benefit of the best opinion available.' An acid smile took the egotism from his words, and he nodded towards Helen Elgin and Shona Bruce. 'The young ladies have already fed me. Now, I suppose, I must earn my keep.'

'I'll show you the way.' Helen Elgin led the professor off in the direction of the laboratory room, leaving Carrick alone with Shona.

'Not at work today?' he asked.

She shook her head. 'Mr Stark telephoned last night. He'd heard about the *Rachel C.* being sunk – he said I wasn't to come in for the rest of the week.'

'Decent of him.'

'Unnecessary. But –' she shrugged – 'that's how it is. Like some coffee?'

'Not just yet.' The telephone was on a low table beside

the big, deep-cushioned couch, and he thumbed towards it. 'Did Blayett call you like he promised?'

'Yes, last night – almost about midnight, in fact.' She rested her hands on her hips. 'He said he'll be sailing later today, but that you're to let him know if he can help.'

'Nice of him,' said Carrick, unable to completely mask his cynicism. 'Did you tell him about Hinton?'

'That he'd been out at my father's place?' She nodded. 'What's going on about Hinton, Webb?'

'Who wants to know, Shona? You – or Blayett?'

A spark of anger kindled in her cat-green eyes. 'I don't think I like that.'

'I didn't imagine you would. Sit down, Shona.'

She did, but reluctantly. 'Well?'

'Somebody tried to kill me last night, and came close to killing the man with me.' He saw her head snap up. Only a professional, a skilled professional, could have duplicated the mute shock on her face. 'If I told you that it came down to whether you are loyal to Helen or to Blayett, which would it be?' Before she could answer, while a retort was still stoking on her lips, he smacked fist on hand. 'I mean it, Shona. Hasn't Blayett been asking questions and been getting answers – from you? Small questions, but persistent, questions that hardly seemed to matter?'

Helen Elgin's return, heralded by the tap of her stiletto heels on the wood-block flooring, saved her friend from an immediate answer.

'I'll get the coffee.' She got up and walked quickly towards the kitchen.

'Been having an argument?' Helen looked at him with resigned good humour. 'Shona's rather short on temper in the morning. I should have warned you.'

'It was more a discussion,' said Carrick. 'I was asking her about Blayett's telephone call.'

'Oh.' She found it unimportant. 'He was pretty disappointed when he found we didn't know where you were.'

133

'That I can believe,' said Carrick dryly. Then, overcoming his own reluctance, 'Helen, did you tell anyone where we were storing our aqualung gear?'

'She told me.' The reply came snapping back from Shona Bruce, standing in the kitchen doorway. She crossed in a brisk, stiff-legged walk and handed him a steaming coffee cup. Her mouth twisted bitterly. 'But before you ask, that's one thing I didn't tell Peter.'

'But I did.' Helen glanced from Shona to Carrick, and flushed. 'It was when we were going out to the Glenconnel, last night – remember, Shona, he picked me up first in town, then we collected you at the Crosslodge gates?'

'Where do we go from there?' The other girl slumped down on the couch. 'You gave me a choice, Webb. All right, Peter Blayett has been asking a lot of questions.' She turned to Helen. 'It seems I've been acting as a microphone around here, the original bush telegraph.' She gave a helpless shrug.

'You mean that Peter Blayett –' Helen Elgin absorbed the shock, then moistened her lips. 'You're sure, Webb?'

'Near enough to sure.' He got to his feet. 'When you got to the hotel last night, did you ever leave him on his own?'

'Well, we were in the powder room for a spell – he went on and organized the table.'

'And could have made a telephone call?'

'A couple, if he'd wanted,' agreed Shona Bruce.

'Then this is even more important. Does he know Professor MacEwan is here?'

'No –' They were positive in their answer.

'Then let's keep it that way.'

'Webb, what about Alex Hinton?' Shona Bruce fumbled for a cigarette from the box on the table, and lit it. 'Mr Stark asked me if I knew any friends of his – when he called me this morning, I mean. When I said I didn't, he just changed the subject.'

'Helen, you'd better sit down too.' Carrick pushed her gently towards the couch. 'I'm going to tell you a little of what's been happening.'

They heard him out, with only an occasional question. Once, as he told how Dr Elgin must have died, he saw Shona's hand go out and rest for a moment on the other girl's wrist.

'Blayett – and our Mr Hinton, wherever he may be.' Shona Bruce let anger at her own part spill into her words. 'I must have been handy to know. Very handy.'

'That's over. But don't freeze him off, Shona,' he warned her. 'Not yet.'

'I won't,' she promised, grinding the cigarette in an ashtray. 'I'll look forward to getting a little of my own back.' She turned. 'Helen, I'm sorry –'

He left them – it seemed best. Going through the house, he knocked on the door of the laboratory, then went in. MacEwan was sitting at the desk, a small row of the specimen jars before him, one hand toying with a long, newly sharpened pencil.

'Any luck, Professor?'

'A little – enough to show a possible pattern,' MacEwan answered. He laid down the pencil. 'Elgin's extramural research seems to have been on two themes, partly inter-linked – the vertical migration of plankton, with a possible relationship to water temperature's effect on marine vege-tation, and the recent appearance of certain unusual marine life in this area. You follow?'

'The basics.' Fishery Protection regularly received the Research branch's bulletins, and one point cropping up more and more was the temperature switch. Ocean cur-rents of warmer water, like the Gulf Stream swinging out of the Florida straits and bending across the Atlantic from Cape Cod, had always had a profound effect on European marine life. But it was accepted now that the pattern was gradually changing, that fish and underwater fauna were on the move, the entire distribution of some species show-ing signs of altering. Fish rarely found on the Scottish coast were making appearances in trawl nets – fish like the Red Band, seen only twice before in a hundred years; big, fleshy bass; cuttlefish; and many smaller varieties.

'It's an important field,' mused MacEwan. 'Important

enough for us to be liaising with the U.S. Coast Guard and their naval research people on the whole Atlantic pattern. But it's hardly a reason for murder.'

'Any indication where he was working – deep water, shallow water, off shore?'

'All three, I'm afraid.' MacEwan pushed one group of specimen jars aside. 'These are purely local samplings, organic material.' He frowned at the remaining group. 'These, on the other hand, are mainly deep-water organisms, one or two of them rather unusual in development. I'd like to know myself just where he obtained them.'

'But you can't tell.' Carrick's optimism evaporated.

'I can't tell,' agreed MacEwan soberly. 'But I do know people who might take you a stage further if you gave them this.' He tapped one of the jars, filled with minute, cell-like creatures. 'Some of these are Calanus plankton, Mr Carrick, favourite food of the herring and the reason why so many fishing boats are in this part of the world. This is a bottom-life sample, from fairly deep water, at least a hundred feet, to judge by some of the cell life present. Notice anything about it?'

Carrick peered at the glass jar. 'No, nothing special.'

'Try again.' MacEwan shook the jar twice, then placed it on the desk. 'These little specks of disturbed sediment?'

He saw them for the first time, a few tiny particles sinking down to rest at the foot of the jar. 'They can help?'

'If you've time to spare and know where to go. Napoleon's hair, Mr Carrick – neutron activation analysis! Remember how the forensic people at Glasgow University took a lock of old Bonaparte's hair a little while back and were able to say he'd absorbed a hefty quantity of arsenic before death? Give them a sample of opium, cocaine, any of these drugs, and they'll tell you the country and area of origin – because of the rare earth characteristics of the soil where the original plant was grown.' He pushed the jar towards Carrick. 'We've been working on another line with the technique lately, coastal geology. Each stretch of coastline has its own characteristics – take the sands at Eigg, in the Hebrides, the famous "singing sands". Silicified wood, in the main. Up near Ullapool, on the other hand, it is mostly nullipore, powdered coralline algae.'

'You mean this sediment could give us an exact location – could tell us where the specimen jar was filled?'

'Well, let's say it would give a choice of possible areas. The technical people will remove the sediment, have it irradiated in a research reactor for a period of thirty minutes, then put it under a machine called a scintillation counter. Heaven knows how the thing works – I leave that type of detail to the mechanics of this world. But the process amounts to making the atoms of the sediment unstable by artificial means, then comparing the readings obtained from the machine with those tabulated for known elements. The sediment's makeup is identified, and all that remains is to check the records for areas with a similar geological pattern.'

'If it works . . .' Carrick stared at the sample jar.

'It works.' MacEwan waved one thin white hand airily. 'Nothing else could on a microscopic quantity of this nature.'

'All right, let's do it. You could make the arrangements, Professor?'

'A phone call would be enough.' MacEwan gave a dry chuckle of satisfaction. 'We're always happy to – ah – guide our colleagues in the Protection branch, Chief Officer. Makes us feel a little more needed, which is always good for the soul. Now, how soon would you deliver the sample? Today? Tomorrow?'

Carrick heard the sound of a car drawing up outside, then the distinctive throb of the Humber's idling engine. 'Within the hour.'

'Hmm. In that case, I'll telephone right away.'

By the time MacEwan had finished his call, Carrick had rearranged his plans. Another phone call, this time to Chief Inspector Deacon, and he was promised a police car and driver. Then it was Clapper Bell's turn.

'The police car will take you and these specimen jars to Glasgow. Wait until the forensic people have finished, and bring the results back down here.'

137

Petty Officer Bell nodded. 'What about the harbour check, sir? Bill Duart's workin' on it now.'

'I'll take care of it.' He turned to the others. 'In fact, I'd better get down there now.'

'Don't worry about me,' said MacEwan. 'The sooner I can get a train back to Edinburgh, the better.'

'We'll wait here until the results arrive,' said Helen Elgin, a growing hope in her eyes. 'Webb, if it comes off –'

'I'll tell you,' he promised.

The police car, a Jaguar, arrived in a matter of minutes. Clapper Bell boarded it, the specimen jars packed carefully in a small cardboard grocery box, and the car swept on its way.

Carrick left a moment later. He dropped MacEwan off at the railway station, then drove on to the port area and parked the department car outside the harbourmaster's office.

Inside, Bill Duart groaned when he saw his visitor. 'Look, Webb, I told your pal this would take time. I'm only getting started!'

'I thought you could maybe use some help.'

'That makes a difference!' Duart brightened. With his good hand he flicked over the pages of the heavy ledger on the desk before him. 'This is our baby – the harbour daybook. Supposing I shout the details, and you do the listing?'

'Suits me.' Carrick pulled in a chair, ready to go to work. 'Much traffic on the move today?'

'Plenty. Everybody's getting out, now the weather has changed – including your pals on the *Karmona*.' Duart searched for his starting place in the list of ship names and dates. 'She's leaving at noon – some of the dockers are taking bets on when she'll be back. The odds are on first thing tomorrow.' He grinned. 'Well, I won't be here to find out. Tomorrow's my day off, and the programme is an extra-long snooze in the morning, then a wander round town in the afternoon with my wife. She's threatening to make me buy a new suit while we're at it. We'll have a meal out somewhere, and maybe take in a cinema. A decent Western would do me –' He glanced up. 'Hey, what's the matter?'

Carrick was staring out of the window, his mind searching for an answer to a hitherto unrealized question. 'I need a new suit too, Bill. I was wondering what will happen to the old one.'

Duart chuckled. 'Probably end up being worn by some scarecrow.'

'Not this one,' said Carrick. 'Can I use your phone?'

'Mind using the one in the back office?' asked Duart. 'I keep this one as clear as possible for harbour calls – anyway, the back office is empty. You'll have more privacy.'

He left Duart, went into the other office, dialled Crosslodge's number, and asked for the Health Unit extension.

Dr Morden was apparently having an idle morning. His voice sounded cheerfully over the line as he took the incoming call, and his worries of the previous day appeared to have evaporated. 'Everybody else is in so big a flap they seem to have forgotten about us,' he confided. 'The longer it stays that way, the better I'll like it.'

'Still got my uniform?' queried Carrick. 'You said it was condemned, but –'

'Sorry, you've seen the last of it,' declared Morden. 'Nothing I can do about it.'

'I don't want it back,' said Carrick patiently. 'But I want to know what's happened to it.'

'Nothing – at least not yet. It's in the solid waste-disposal area. Next time there's a load gathered, it'll be dumped.'

'Dumped where?'

'In a nice deep part of the ocean, inside a large dustbin with a reinforced concrete jacket.'

'That's standard practice?'

'It has to be. In some parts of the world they use old coal mines for their solid waste. It can be all sorts of junk, from filters and laboratory equipment at the one end of the scale to nasty items like caesium and strontium at the other. But if you're near the sea, you don't look further.'

'One of the Authority ships takes the stuff out?'

'That's right – the *Fermia*.' Morden's manner changed a little. 'No need to worry about your fish, Mr Carrick. We take plenty of precautions.'

'I'm not worried, just interested,' Carrick told him. 'How often is the waste taken out – and where is it dumped?'

'Well, the *Fermia* comes in about once every three weeks, and she took on the last load – oh, about three nights ago,' said Morden casually. 'I don't know the exact dumping area, but I can find out if you want.'

'I'd like that.' Carrick gave him the harbour-office number, and hung up. His next call, to the main coastguard station at Portpatrick, on the busy main west coast shipping route, took a little longer. Once he'd been connected, minutes ticked past while the coastguard unit checked through their lists of ship sightings. At last they had what he wanted – the last four dates for the *Fermia*, all at regular three-week intervals, all sightings as she headed north, none for her return south.

Wherever the *Fermia* dumped her cargo, it left her with a course for home which steered well clear of the normal sea route.

'Funny you should ask about her,' volunteered the coast-guard. 'We had a report about her yesterday morning – she'd been sheltering off Campbeltown Loch until the storm blew over. But she'll be on her way by now.'

Carrick thanked him, hung up, and went back to the outer office. 'Here's a new approach, Bill. Four dates – I want the names of every ship coming or going from port round about that time. Let's say three days on either side.'

They set to work. First came the full list, then the discarding of some vessels in the passenger-ferry class, followed by names which only featured on one of the dated sectors and a few other obvious rejections.

'Just two left,' said Carrick softly when they'd finished. 'The *Karmona* is always in port before these dates, and leaves a day later.' In port before the nuclear-waste collection ship arrived off Crosslodge, out again the day after the waste ship must have sailed from the power station, bound for her dumping ground!

'This one, the *Bennici* – what do you know about her?'

'A tramp freighter, pretty small.' Duart rubbed his chin. 'Panamanian registered – the old flag-of-convenience racket – about 1500 tons.'

'And she always sails two days after the *Karmona*! What's her usual cargo?'

Duart consulted his lists. 'Brings in general cargo from the Mediterranean, takes out scrap steel. What goes on anyway, Webb?'

'Scavengers,' murmured Carrick to the room in general. 'Ruddy scavengers. Going through the garbage bins, because they've been guaranteed good pickings.'

'Garbage? What garbage?' The harbourmaster shook his head. 'Look, Webb, I don't know what's going on in that tiny mind of yours, but your pattern isn't running true. The *Karmona* and the *Bennici* are both in port right now. But they're both due to sail at noon.'

That fitted too – the waste-collection ship had been delayed by the storm, so the *Karmona* had faked yet another engine breakdown. But the *Bennici*, once she'd loaded, would have to stick to schedule. Any delaying tactics on her part might attract attention. The next step – he reached for the telephone on Duart's desk, then stopped as the instrument began ringing.

'I'll get it.' Duart flipped the receiver from its rest with his iron hook and propped it between his left ear and shoulder. 'Harbour office.' He listened, and glanced towards Carrick. 'Yes, he's here.' With his right hand, he passed the receiver across. 'For you. A woman.'

'Thanks.' Carrick answered the call.

'Webb? It's Shona here.' Her voice was oddly strained. 'Can you come out to the house, now, right away?'

'If it's important – why, what's happened?' he asked.

'Those missing pages from Dr Elgin's diary – Helen has just found them. Will you come?'

'Yes.' His grip on the receiver tightened. 'I'll be straight over. Where were they?'

'We'll explain when you come.' She hung up, and the line went dead.

It took him four minutes in the Humber to get out to the Elgin house. He ran up the front pathway, saw the opened door, went in – then came to a sudden halt.

Peter Blayett was there, a stubby Mauser automatic in one hand, the muzzle pointing unwaveringly towards Carrick's midriff.

Chapter Seven

'Shut the door – use your right foot, don't hurry it, and don't try to be a hero.' The Mauser's round black muzzle stared at him like a single hungry eye, and the trawler skipper's face was as cold and emotionless as a wall of rock. Blayett was standing just within the shadow of the cloakroom doorway, and across the hallway, by the lounge door, another figure had appeared, a small fat man who wore a blue woollen skullcap. A swarthy little man, middle-aged, with quick, nervous eyes, almost a comical little man, until you noted the Parabellum Luger in his grip and realized that this gun, too, wasn't wavering a fraction from its target.

Carrick eased the door shut behind him, heard the lock click, and saw Blayett give an almost imperceptible nod of approval. 'Through to the room, Carrick. We've a schedule to maintain, and you're part of it.'

The fat man stood back to let Carrick enter.

'Webb!' Helen Elgin started to rise from her chair by the fireplace. She was unhurt, unmarked – he saw that, then she was thrust back down again by the tall, saturnine-faced trawler hand who stood behind her. Shona Bruce was there too, white-faced, sitting in another chair opposite. The gun in their guard's hand was reason enough for them letting Carrick blunder in without warning.

'The last member of our party,' said Blayett with a purr of satisfaction. 'Look him over, Benny.'

The fat man grunted and carefully, working at arm's length, made a quick but thorough search. He extracted

Carrick's wallet and clasp knife and was satisfied. 'Nothing else, skipper.'

'Good.' Blayett used his free hand to light a cigarette, watchful throughout. 'Not going to ask why, Carrick?'

'I can think of several reasons,' said Carrick grimly. 'People beginning to breathe too closely down your neck, Blayett?'

'Let's say you are,' corrected the trawler skipper. 'So now we're taking you out of circulation for a spell. Palmer –' the second trawler hand glanced his way – 'help the ladies get their coats. They won't make trouble, not when their friend takes the consequences.'

Palmer grinned. 'Move.' He gave Shona Bruce a vicious, unexpected shove which sent her sprawling from the chair, landing on hands and knees. Helen Elgin helped her up, and both girls were pushed on out of the room.

'The phone call was a fake, of course,' said Blayett conversationally. 'It wasn't easy – my Shona took a little more persuading than I'd anticipated, even with a gun against her brunette friend's pretty ear.'

Carrick didn't answer. He'd fallen for an old, old trick, and he felt sick at the knowledge.

'Like to tell me how far you'd got?' Blayett shrugged. 'Well, we'll have time to find out.'

In a moment the two girls and their guard were back in the room. Carrick felt the sickness within him turn to mounting wrath as he saw the fresh red blotch that marked Helen Elgin's left cheek and jaw.

'Didn't like me looking through her handbag,' said Palmer laconically. 'I belted her one.'

'And we're ready.' Blayett took a last look around before he gestured towards the door. 'Carrick, you first. We'll travel in your car, and I don't need to tell you to behave.'

'Where's the M.G.?' If Deacon's men were still on shadowing detail, there was a hope remaining. But the hope died as Blayett shook his head.

'Still at the harbour – too conspicuous. This was rather a special trip, quickly arranged. Let's just say we acquired transport.'

Six was a squeeze in the Humber, too much of a squeeze to allow room for any kind of manoeuvre, especially with Helen sitting between him and Blayett, Blayett's gun muzzle jammed just below her ribs. Carrick obeyed orders, drove quietly through the town and into the harbour area, and parked the department car as he was told behind a dock warehouse a little way from the *Karmona*'s berth.

'Benny –' Blayett jerked his head towards the back of the car. 'You know what to bring. Now listen, you three. You're going to walk over to the *Karmona* with me, a nice, friendly quartet. If your imagination starts working, just remember Benny and Palmer are behind us.'

Their last chance disappeared as they crossed the quayside to the trawler. The few dockers in sight were busy round a newly berthed coaster, and paid no attention. There was *Snapper*, such a short distance away – but the rating standing guard by the fishery cruiser's gangway had his back towards them. Carrick glanced at Blayett as they walked on, saw a twitch of tension in one corner of his mouth, and knew that the man was at a pitch where the slightest alarm would bring explosive reaction . . . and then they were clambering aboard the trawler.

'Straight below with them.' The words sighed from Blayett like the release of pressure from a valve. He turned away, striding towards the wheelhouse. Around them, the *Karmona*'s deck crew were already at their stations, the trawler's engine was throbbing, the steel deck plates vibrating to its pulse. A sea-booted trawlerman jumped to the quayside, ready to cast off the mooring lines.

'You – down.' Palmer's automatic prodded Carrick towards a short, steep companionway ladder. He climbed down, into the small, damp-smelling messroom below, where a third cold-faced deck hand was waiting. The others followed – first Benny, breathing heavily through his mouth, then Helen and Shona, finally Palmer. Above them, feet were pattering on the trawler's deck and Blayett's voice shouted unintelligible orders.

Benny crossed to the far corner of the messroom, opened a door, and gestured to Carrick again. 'Inside.'

'All right.' Carrick took his time about obeying. 'Still losing your hair, Benny? Do you know the reason?' He saw the fat trawlerhand's mouth tremble, and knew he'd struck home. 'Radiation sickness, isn't it? Noticed how you tire out more easily? Want to know why?'

'It can wait.' The fat man's voice was strained. 'Turn round.'

'Can it?' Carrick turned slowly, knowing what was coming. He part sensed, part saw, the gun turn in the other man's hand, the upward sweep of the arm, the start of the downward stroke. Then the butt of the gun hit him hard in the nape of the neck, and he buckled.

He came round in what was little bigger than a store cupboard – a small, stale-aired, windowless, steel-walled cabin, its sole furnishing the bare wooden boards of the bunk on which he was lying. A low-power electric bulb shone down from the ceiling, and the *Karmona* was alive with all the shuddering creaks and groans of a vessel at sea. Her engine pounded steadily, pounded in rhythm, with the thumping pain spread across his skull. He winced, started to rise, and a pair of slim, strong arms helped him sit upright.

'Don't rush it,' advised Helen Elgin. 'Shona –'

'Try this.' The other girl moved across his red-hazed vision. Something which was wonderfully cold, damp, but heavily perfumed was placed across his forehead.

He sniffed, and his eyes watered. 'What's that you're using?'

'All we've got – pure cologne on a handkerchief.' Helen Elgin fought the anxiety in her voice. 'How do you feel?'

'Horrible.' Carrick swung his legs experimentally over the edge of the bunk, let his body rock with the trawler's motion for a moment, then, his head spinning, forced a far from happy grin. 'How long have I been out?'

'Twenty minutes.' Shona Bruce glanced at her wrist watch. 'It's not quite noon yet.'

He groaned again, felt better for it, searched his pockets,

and found his cigarettes and lighter. He lit one, and the tobacco smoke cleared the last of the haze from his head, leaving only the persistent thumping pain. 'Have I missed much?'

Nothing, they told him. From the moment he'd been knocked out and they'd been shoved into the cabin, the door locked from the outside, they'd been left completely alone.

'Who got me on the bunk?' It didn't seem in character for either Benny or Palmer to devote time to lifting him off the deck.

'We did.' Helen Elgin ran a hand over her brow at the recollection. 'You're no lightweight – we nearly gave up.'

'Webb –' Shona Bruce stepped between them. 'About that telephone call . . .' Her eyes were bright with anxiety.

'Blayett told me,' Carrick soothed her. 'You hadn't any choice, Shona.' But if the call had been even two minutes later, and he'd had a chance to contact Deacon first, even tell Bill Duart what he'd uncovered and what he'd guessed as a result, he'd have felt very much different about their immediate prospects.

'Blayett came to the door first, alone,' said Helen bitterly. 'Then the other two arrived – we couldn't do a thing.'

'There's no sense pretending.' Shona Bruce sat dispirited on the far end of the bunk. 'We're here, and he can do what he likes.' She looked up. 'But why – why bring us here? What's the sense of it?'

'Because I was suddenly too close to too many answers,' said Carrick. 'You were a lever to get me. But once he'd used you, you couldn't be left behind.'

'You mean you'd found the truth?' Helen Elgin gripped his arm. 'Webb, does anyone else –'

He shook his head. 'Nobody else has it, Helen. Call it sheer bad luck. No, we've just one chance of outside help, those specimen jars Clapper Bell took to Glasgow. It's slim –'

'And it's hopeless,' said Shona Bruce dully. 'Why don't you say it, admit it?' Her hands lay clenched on her lap.

'Do you think Blayett and Hinton will treat us any different from the way they treated Helen's father – or my uncle and the two men with him?'

'Perhaps.' Carrick tried to inject some confidence. 'Things are different. They know their play's just about over – the *Karmona*'s on its way out to collect one last load. There won't be any more – Blayett knows that. He won't be coming back.' He prowled across to the door.

It was held by a modern spring lock, hard to pick, even with proper tools. 'They'll be back before long. Let's see what we've got between us.'

He emptied his own pockets on to the bunk boards – money, cigarettes and lighter, handkerchief and pen – no, not a pen. It was the miniaturized Geiger counter he'd borrowed from Crosslodge. He put it back in his inside pocket, and watched while Helen Elgin followed his example, emptying her handbag.

Shona did the same, moving woodenly, reluctantly, as if already resigned to fate. The collection was slim. Palmer had been thorough in his check before they'd left the house. He'd hoped for scissors, perhaps a nail file, but neither remained.

Carrick lit another cigarette from the stub of the first, and considered their total armoury. Two pencils and a small pencil sharpener lay beside Shona Bruce's powder compact and purse. He broke several fingernails before he managed to loosen the single screw which held the inch-long sliver of edged-steel blade to the sharpener's case, then carefully used the blade to prise loose the compact's mirror.

'Any of your cologne left?'

Helen nodded. About a tablespoonful remained, and he slipped the little bottle into one pocket, put the mirror in the other, then told them to repack the rest.

As they did, he looked at the little blade in his hand, then at the door. There wasn't a chance that way – but the blade might still have its uses. He eased it in beneath the leather of his watch strap, then tightened the strap a notch for safety's sake.

Another hour passed before a key turned in the lock and the door was thrown open. Benny stood in the doorway, in no hurry to come in, gun in hand and another crewman in attendance behind him.

'Wide awake again, Mister?' The small fat man gave a loose-lipped snigger. 'Well, you're for a stroll on deck – skipper's orders.' But he shook his head as Helen Elgin instinctively reached for her handbag. 'Not you two – this is just for the Fishery snoop.'

'I'll be back.' Carrick wasn't so sure about that, but he said it anyway. Benny stepped back to let him out, then slammed and locked the cabin door before motioning Carrick across the messroom to the companionway behind.

On deck, Carrick steadied himself against the *Karmona*'s pitching roll and took a deep, thankful breath of the clean air. One or two of the trawler's crew were at work around, the nearest of them, young, unshaven, and pimple-faced, leaning back against her winch to examine him with all the interest of an adolescent cat considering a captive mouse.

The *Karmona* was making about fourteen knots through a moderate sea. The hazing mist was still around, but a great hulking fortress of granite rock, jutting high, grey and phantomlike astern, gave him an immediate bearing. They were off Ailsa Craig, the strange, almost perpendicular hump of rock which hulks 1100 feet high as a solitary guardian to the mouth of the Firth of Clyde. Deserted except for lighthouse keepers and the workmen who came out to cut chunks of her granite heart to fashion into curling stones that went wherever the roaring game was played, Ailsa Craig was ten miles out from the mainland – and their present course could be the first wide curve of a route round the Mull of Kintyre, out beyond the grave of the *Rachel C.*

'Never mind the view,' grunted Benny, pushing him on. 'Get up for'ard.'

Blayett was there, dressed in a sweater and heavy serge trousers like the rest of his men, an old gabardine jacket hanging loose from his shoulders. He gave a curt nod.

'Not another ship in sight, Carrick. Not a radio message mentioning us – it looks like nobody's missed you yet.' He reached out and rubbed one hand thoughtfully along the painted surface of the trawler's foremast. 'That's the way I want things, trouble free. You came close to spoiling the picture, didn't you?'

'By finding out about the *Fermia*?' Carrick shrugged. There was no bonus to be gained in denials. 'Yes, I was close enough. Who tipped you off?'

Blayett viewed him sardonically. 'Always the sea-going cop – Carrick, it's a waste of time. Don't press your luck.' His manner hardened. 'How many fishery cruisers are operating in the west area?'

'Four.'

'Too quick, a little too quick for truth.' Blayett's hand swept from the mast and hit Carrick a hard, jarring blow across the mouth. It drew blood where the upper lip was cut against teeth. 'Try again, and this time I want names.'

The fishing grapevine would be at work anyway. Carrick saw no reason to prolong matters. '*Snapper* is in harbour at Ayr, *Skua* and *Marlin* are on patrol. That's the lot.'

Blayett looked at him for a moment, and appeared satisfied. '*Snapper* won't bother us. When she tries to leave harbour, they're going to find a length of old wire cable has somehow fouled around her starboard screw. The word is out that one fishery cruiser is to the south, off the Wigtown coast, and another is north, off Arran. All nicely out of the way.' His smile was with lips and teeth alone. 'Carrick, if there was a fourth prowling around, and it appeared at the wrong moment, neither you nor these two below would be aboard by the time it came alongside. You understand?'

'There are only the three.'

'Let's hope so.' The trawler skipper nodded to Carrick's escort. 'Take him back down.'

'Blayett –' Carrick stood his ground, ignoring the Parabellum's muzzle grinding into his backbone.

'Well?' A finger signalled to the fat, skull-capped deck hand, and the pressure eased.

150

'What happens to us once you've trawled up the waste containers and collected the fuel cartridges?'

'I wondered when you'd ask.' Blayett regarded him without emotion or antagonism. 'Once we've done, the *Karmona* simply disappears –'

'And us? Do we end up like the *Rachel C.*'s crew and Helen's father?'

'No, not necessarily.' Blayett swayed with the trawler as a larger wave broke on their port quarter, drenching the deck with spray. 'We were forced into both of those.' He treated the matter as calmly as if discussing the day's fishing prospects. 'Old Elgin's damned researching was his own death warrant. He wanted to do some private sampling near the dump area – even asked me if I'd take him out. When I said no, he fixed up with his pal Bruce on the *Rachel C.*'

'But it was his bad luck they turned up out there at the wrong time, after the last dumping?'

'Right. Maybe they didn't know what we were up to, but the old fellow was peeved at me first refusing to take him then going out myself. We had to do something before he moaned to somebody who might be – well, even more curious.' Blayett shrugged. 'We wouldn't have bothered with the line-boat, but Joe Bruce caught too many good fish out there while Elgin was sampling. He'd been going back out on his own, and it was becoming awkward.'

'So you let him get his catch two nights back, let him start for home with the storm blowing up – then rammed him.'

'Right again. We were buying time, Carrick. Time, and a trouble-free last trip.'

'Just like you fixed the air tanks on our aqualungs?'

'The same.' Blayett was curious. 'You did try to check our hull last night, didn't you?' He accepted Carrick's tightened mouth as confirmation. 'We saw one man in the water – you must have been lucky. Still, it was a waste of time. This old tub's got a bow that could slice through any line-boat going, and never bear the mark.' He'd grown

151

tired of the conversation. 'Let's say you three are insurance, Carrick, insurance against trouble. If everything goes smoothly, we'll be within a day's sailing to any of the Hebridean Isles. Ever read Robinson Crusoe? I hope so – I'm planning to shove you ashore on a nicely isolated, uninhabited island. There are plenty to choose from – and if you're lucky, you'll be picked up within a week or so. If you're not, well, life is a gamble.'

He turned abruptly away, and Benny's gun rammed back into position. Carrick trudged aft without waiting for the order. They'd been given their lives – or had they? It was true, out of the five hundred scattered islands of the Hebrides, only about one in seven is inhabited, the rest deserted and seldom visited. But it wasn't nearly so sweet and simple as it might appear. Plenty of the Hebridean group were mere pinpricks of rock and moss and seaweed, without water or shelter, separated from their kindlier neighbours by savage currents. Even some of the bigger, the inhabited islands, could be cut off from the outside world for weeks on end by rough weather. But did Blayett mean it anyway? Carrick had his own idea about what might happen once the last ounce of potential usefulness had been extracted from them.

'Hold on.' Benny stopped him at the top of the companionway ladder and called down. There was no answer from below, and he squinted across to the pudgy-faced deck hand at the winch. 'Seen Bolo comin' up, Charlie?'

The younger man nodded. 'He's over at the trawl gear, Benny. Need some help?'

'Of course he does,' said Carrick cynically. He laughed, a forced, harsh sound as a gossamer-thin chance spun before him. 'Benny's the nervous type. Come and help him hold his gun steady.'

'Huh.' The deck hand wiped the sleeve of his jersey across his mouth, enjoying the taunt. 'Maybe you're right. Want a nursemaid, Benny?'

'Why not?' urged Carrick. 'Come on, Benny, it's safe now.'

The fat man's face trembled. 'I can manage this funny

character on my own,' he said huskily. 'Get down, Mister. Then back against the faraway bulkhead, or maybe I'll show you just how clever you are.'

He clambered below, weaved his way past the plain scrubbed table and benches of the messroom and stopped where he'd been told. His guard followed down the ladder, moving clumsily, one hand on the rungs, the other holding the automatic ready. Carrick reached into his pocket and very carefully, very slowly so that no mistakes could be made, took out the Geiger counter.

'How about a deal, Benny?' He held the little instrument in the palm of his hand. 'Know what this is?'

The fat man peered across the gloom. 'I don't need no pens, Mister. Jus' stay back there till I open that door.'

'It's a Geiger counter,' said Carrick softly. 'You know what that means?' He saw the other man hesitate. 'Benny, you'd better listen. It was a chunk of your hair I tore loose outside the girl's house, wasn't it? You've had a radiation dose, and recently. Don't you want to know how bad it is?'

'I know.' The fat man licked his lips. 'The skipper's checked. He'll have me fixed up wit' treatment once this trip's over.' But he took a step nearer, hooked. All that remained was to land him.

'How'd it happen? Did one of the waste containers spring a leak – or did you find it had smashed open when you fished it up?' Carrick sized the man up, and shook his head. 'You weren't diving, that's for sure. You're too old for the game.'

'I was diving all right, Mister, and –' Benny's mouth shut again like a trap. Then his little eyes gleamed balefully. 'Hand it over.'

'The deal is –'

'There's no deal.' The deck hand shambled nearer. 'The skipper wants you alive – but that doesn't mean I can't put a bullet in you where it'll hurt, an' say you started a roughhouse.' He jerked the gun suggestively. 'Put that gadget on the deck halfway between us, then get back.'

Carrick let his shoulders sag, sighed, and obeyed. Benny

153

came forward, stooped down, eyes and gun still on Carrick, and groped with his other hand until he'd found the little instrument. He rose again, examined the Geiger without relaxing his vigilance, then used finger and thumb to pull off his skullcap.

Beneath, the mousey hair grew in rough, isolated patches, separated one from the other by the pale, shroud-white skin of his scalp. He ran the Geiger over his head, and glared accusingly. 'It doesn't work.'

'There's a switch – it's battery-powered. I'll show you.' Carrick edged forward.

'Far enough, Mister.' The fat man swallowed hard. 'Jus' tell me.'

'A switch is built into the clip. Push it down, and run the nib end over the contaminated area. There's a light bulb at the clip end, and it'll begin blinking. You'll hear a very faint clicking, and you'll get an exact reading from the calibrated dial.' Carrick put his hands in his pockets, the left seeking the tiny cologne bottle, unscrewing the cap. 'The principle's simple – a tube of gas which only conducts current when radiation is present.'

Benny nodded, his fingers trembling as he pushed the switch. The light began flashing immediately, the rate increasing as gradually, reluctantly, hypnotized by the warning pulse of the voice of the atom, he moved it nearer to his head.

'Check the reading,' rapped Carrick suddenly.

The man's whole attention swung towards the Geiger's dial for a space of seconds, enough for Carrick to lunge forward. His left hand flung the last of the cologne into Benny's eyes. The right grabbed the gun, twisting it aside, simultaneously seeking, gripping and levering back the top joint of the trigger finger before the trawlerman's reflexes could operate.

The twin shock of pain and attack took Benny off balance. The Geiger fell to the deck, his free hand clawed instinctively towards his stinging eyes, his mouth opened, in a half-framed bellow of rage. Then Carrick's left fist hit him below the ear, every ounce of muscle he possessed behind the crunching blow. The fat man folded and went limp, his shout strangling at its opening gasp.

Carrick eased him floorward, crouched down beside him, and, after a quick glance towards the hatchway, pulled the Parabellum free and nursed its hard, squat shape, in his right hand. Blood flowed between the clenched fingers of his other fist. He'd still gripped the tiny perfume bottle when he'd struck that knockout blow, and the jarring force had smashed the phial, its fragmented glass cutting into the flesh in half a dozen places.

The cabin key – he switched the Parabellum to his left hand, wincing at the contact, reached to feel the man's pockets, then instinctively glanced up again towards the companionway hatch.

His eyes met a pudgy, pimpled face which gaped in surprise. Then the deck hand above had a gun in his hand – and Carrick triggered the Parabellum.

A Parabellum Luger fires a .22 bullet, small, but backed by high velocity. The cupro-nickel slug took the man high in the right shoulder, and the deck hand jerked a split second before his own gun blasted wild. But the bullet still found a target, and the unconscious Benny was the mark.

There were shouts and the thud of running feet from the deck above. The pudgy face had disappeared from the hatchway, and the two girls in the locked cabin were calling his name, their fists hammering on the other side of the metal door. Carrick found the key in Benny's hip pocket, saw another head appear at the companionway, blasted a fast shot in that direction, and the hatchway space was quickly vacated. Still in his crouch, he moved across to the door. He had the key in the lock, was still trying to think even one step, one move ahead in the powderkeg situation, when he heard a creak of hinges from behind him. A warm, oily draught of air touched his neck.

'Stay perfectly still, Carrick.' Blayett's voice echoed in the messroom's confines, deadly in intent. He froze, the gun still in his hand.

'Here's a warning.' A gun roared behind him, the bullet smashed against the steel deck plates inches from his feet, and performed a mad double ricochet. Above, two new heads made a cautious appearance at the companionway hatch, two more gun muzzles peered down at him.

'Now get rid of it.'

Carrick pushed the little automatic away, brought his hand back empty, then rose to his feet and turned. Blayett and the tall, saturnine Palmer stood in an opened doorway behind him – a small, steel doorway which gave a glimpse of machinery beyond. They'd ducked down through the engineroom to get to him – and he'd lost.

They pushed him up the companionway to the open deck, where he ran a cuffing, kicking gauntlet of angry crewmen. But there was brief satisfaction in the sight of Charlie, who sat huddled, moaning and clutching a blood-stained towel to his shoulder. Forced back against the deckhouse, Carrick watched Blayett approach, the trawler skipper's face stony and expressionless, but his eyes black pits of anger.

'You stupid young moron!' Blayett ground out the words and flung them at the wounded deck hand. 'You know what you managed to do down there? You shot Benny, you gun-happy idiot – and he's dead.'

'Which makes one diver less for the transfer,' mumbled Carrick through battered lips. 'That's how it's done, isn't it?'

'That's how it's done.' Blayett glared at him. 'I might have given you that chance on an island, Carrick – I just might. But not now, not you.' He gestured to Palmer. 'Bring the gear – and have somebody get that whimpering fool down to his bunk.'

Two of them dragged the wounded deck hand away. Palmer came back in a moment, a hungry, anticipatory twist to his lips as he dumped a canvas holdall on the deck. Now Carrick knew the reason for Blayett's cryptic order as they'd left the department car back at the harbour – his own aqualung kit lay in front of him.

'You never did hear how Dr Elgin died,' said Blayett

156

softly. 'Well, I'll tell you. We shoved him down in the fish hold – which is how he picked up that radiation contamination, a backwash of what happened to Benny when we were unloading one of the drums and found it was cracked. We topped up his air cylinders with carbon dioxide, left them handy, then let him escape. He went over the side two miles off shore, and we pretended to go looking for him, kept him under – we knew five minutes would be enough.' He shook his head. 'But that's not for you, Carrick. I brought your stuff along to make it look like you were out snooping somewhere, but Palmer has a better idea. A much better idea – and Palmer and Benny were partners.'

The circle of men around them edged nearer. Above the trawler's foremast, a hovering seabird gave a shrill squawk and planed off on an up current of wind.

'We're starting trawling, for appearances' sake – and there's four hundred feet of water under us.' Blayett prodded the holdall with one foot. 'Nobody has tampered with these cylinders, Carrick. But you're going to get into your outfit, and we're going to trawl you in that net. We'll be bottom trawling. Your gear's good for a maximum of two hundred feet – the rest is your problem.'

It was a sentence of death.

The executioner wouldn't be depth. The human body can withstand the crushing pressure of deep water to a fantastic degree – the tables he'd had to memorize at naval diving school swept across his mind like so many illuminated signs. Breathing special oxygen-and-gas mixtures under compression, man had been to below 1000 feet without armoured protection. But with Carrick's straightforward compressed-air aqualung, nitrogen narcosis, the killer rapture of the deep, lay in wait below the two-hundred-foot mark.

It would come on gradually at first, the strange, not fully understood reaction which followed the absorption under pressure of the nitrogen which makes up almost four fifths of the earth's atmosphere. Carrick, like most skin divers, had tasted it before. He'd felt suddenly happy and confident, then merry to a point of drunkenness – and he'd got up fast towards the safety of a lesser depth when the first hint of hysterical loss of reasoning had nudged at his mind, a loss that had caused some divers in the past to deliberately remove their breathing apparatus, others to lose all sense of direction, time or purpose before swift unconsciousness drifted into death.

Nitrogen narcosis could kill. At four hundred feet, it would.

Five men fought him down, half-stunned him before they could forcibly dress him in the diving rubbers and aqualung rig. They searched his clothes as they stripped him, and the tiny compact mirror brought him another kick from Palmer before it was tossed over the side.

But in the first moments of the struggle, when he was knocked to the deck, Carrick rolled face down, sheltering his head in his arms – for just long enough to transfer the little steel sharpener blade from its hiding place beneath the wrist-watch strap into his mouth, pushed down between his cheek and lower jaw. It meant hope, and Carrick's remaining struggles were window dressing while he husbanded strength for the inevitable ahead.

The final item of the process was the fastening of his depth gauge to one arm, a minor refinement which was a leering afterthought by one of the five. The trawl was already on the gallows boom, positioned for lowering, and the *Karmona* had slowed to little more than a crawl.

They thrust him bodily into the trawl's mouth, cursing and pushing to move him deeper down as the aqualung gear tangled with the coarse mesh of the net. Blayett came to look at him, coldly indifferent, the anger gone from his face. He gave a nod, but didn't stay to see the rest. He strode off towards the *Karmona*'s wheelhouse as the winch began to whine.

The gallows boom swung, the trawl began to stream, and Carrick had a last tangled view of trawler and sky before the net was going down, taking him with it, the green water closing over his head while the great trawl bag began unfolding and spreading its width.

He used the first few seconds to adjust his breathing apparatus and face mask, blowing extra air into the mask to force out the lingering sea water. Four hundred feet – he reckoned it would take about five minutes for the trawl to reach that depth, in part due to the pace at which the long wire warps would be paid out from the *Karmona*'s winches, the rest dictated by the net's rate of sinking. Five minutes – that meant he'd probably a maximum of three and a half in which to work. Trawling at a speed of at least six knots, the net was moving too quickly for him to swim out of the bag. Clawing a way along the moving mesh, against the force of the water, would be equally impossible.

Already, the first few fish to be harvested, small, silvery mackerel, were darting around him in a furious, fruitless search for escape . . . the sight jerked him to action.

He freed himself from the last entanglement of the net's mesh, kicked loose, and finned round until he was facing up towards the top of the bag. As the net continued to spread around him, its final cone approaching, he chose his spot, shot up, and gripped the mesh. He glanced at the depth gauge – ninety feet, standard pressure forty pounds per square inch.

Carrick took a deep breath, held it, removed his mouthpiece, and, air bubbling from his lips, got a finger-and-thumb grip on the thin sliver of steel. He drew it out, replaced the mouthpiece, then knew a moment of near horror as, changing his grip, he nearly lost the inch-long blade. But he held it, locked it between his fingers, and began sawing at the tough cord, concentrating on cutting a single slit through these squares of five-inch-wide mesh.

The steel was sharp, but the salt-water-saturated cords were tough and his fingers cold and clumsy in their grip. His heart was pounding, it was a major discipline to breathe slowly and regularly, and a stab of pain behind his right eye reminded him of another peril. He twisted his mouth and forced compressed air into the facepiece to equalize the building outer pressure. Water seeped back in with the air, half-flooding the facepiece, but the real danger was avoided; there was pressure inside his body, pressure from the air cylinders, regulated to meet the outside water pressure. But the pressure under the facepiece had been less than either – and the body pressure had begun pushing behind his eyes.

At the 200-foot mark, the safety limit, his gap in the trawl net was about two feet long. The light filtering down from the surface had changed to a dull blue, and bigger fish were drifting past him as he worked – herring and cod, a large and angry dogfish which cannoned off his legs, skate, and haddock.

A new, relaxed confidence enveloped him, and he fought it off, knowing what it meant. Time was running out.

Mustering concentration, growing progressively light-headed, he sawed through two more of the mesh cords, at a different angle. Depth 260 feet, fingers slowing, an idiotic, giggling mood creeping up on him – he reckoned he might take 300 feet, but no more. Another cord, halfway through – through.

His escape flap complete, Carrick eased his shoulders through the gap, jerked free by brute force as one of the air bottles snagged an uncut mesh, and kicked upwards, rising steadily, but restraining a desperate urge to head straight for the surface. The last of the trawl went rippling past beneath him, the final cone a writhing, bewildered mass of trapped life.

At the 200-foot minimum safety mark, he halted the ascent and floated, barely moving, allowing his head to begin to clear and his senses to return to normal. That done, the rest was a discipline of gradually rising at a rate slower than his own air bubbles, using the depth gauge to choose decompression stops. He wanted those stops, not because they were physically necessary but for their time-consuming value.

Carrick's head broke surface after twelve minutes. He

160

bobbed with a wave, looked from its crest, saw the *Karmona* still steaming on, already a faint blur almost a mile away, and was satisfied. They'd probably wait another fifteen minutes before they hauled in the trawl and found the cut in the net. To backtrack in this deceptive mist, locate one pinpoint of a head in such an expanse of open sea – it was close to impossible.

But he swam for another half hour, always ready to go down again. Then, tiring, he dumped his weight belt, cracked the little CO_2 capsule built within his suit, and inflated its self-contained life-jacket.

That done, he lay back and let the sea have its will.

Carrick had been four numbing hours in the water when the trawler came alongside and he was pulled aboard. He lay on the deck, hardly moving, hardly caring, until a savage slash of brandy poured down his throat. It burned life back into him, he coughed, looked up, and managed a feeble grin.

'Mamma,' said Hendrick Munsen. 'Do we keep this one, or do we throw him back?'

'This one we keep,' said his wife. Her massive arms gathered Carrick up as another woman would a child. 'A good catch, eh, Hendrick?'

Together, they carried him in to the warmth of the *Tecta*.

Chapter Eight

On the chart, the *Tecta*'s position was eight miles south-west of the Mull of Kintyre. Above, the sky was already dusking while a chill, freshening northerly wind had chased the last traces of mist and now teased fine curtains of white spume from the wavecaps around. The trawler was alone – until 1800 hours, when *Marlin*'s silhouette began to grow on her horizon.

From the trawler, Webb Carrick watched the fishery cruiser close the distance and was puzzled. On his feet again, dressed in a borrowed jersey and slacks, knowing exhaustion but fighting it off, he knew less than an hour had passed since the *Tecta*'s radio had pumped out a call on the priority frequency he'd given Hendrick Munsen. *Marlin* shouldn't have been due for another couple of hours . . .

Another surprise came fast. As the two vessels came alongside, the *Tecta*'s old motor-tyre fenders bumping gently against *Marlin*'s spick-and-span hemp, the first man to jump the gap from the fishery cruiser was Commander Dobie, followed by Clapper Bell and Captain Shannon.

'Never heard of helicopters, young fellow?' asked Dobie moments later. Obviously pleased with himself, he settled back in the big, old-fashioned armchair in the Munsens' cabin and glanced around. 'Well, looks like we owe the *Tecta* a vote of thanks, eh, Shannon?'

'Aye.' *Marlin*'s captain glanced sourly at Munsen and gave a reluctant nod. 'Seems so.'

Hendrick Munsen sucked his straggling moustache and shrugged. 'Most guests we welcome, Captain Shannon.'

'Welcome is the word.' Carrick fended off Mamma Munsen's attempt to feed him another tumbler of the *Tecta*'s potent brandy, then turned back towards Dobie. 'What about the *Karmona*, sir?'

'That's my question too.' Dobie frowned. 'As far as we're concerned, two and two don't make four yet. Our answer is nearer to three and a half – and most of the arithmetic stems from Petty Officer Bell.'

Carrick raised an eyebrow towards Bell, who seemed not the least embarrassed at the praise. 'The sediment samples paid off?'

'In part.' Dobie, at any rate, had no objection to the brandy issue. He swallowed from his tumbler, a startled look came into his eyes, and he touched his lips lightly with his forefingers. 'Unbelievable!' He cleared his throat and blinked. 'Well, let's hear your side, Chief Officer.'

'Sir?' Captain Shannon glanced significantly towards the Munsens, but Dobie shook his head.

'Won't do any harm. Go on, Carrick.'

He told them, from his hunch about the dump ship to the two girls left aboard the *Karmona*, fatigue forgotten, his voice a flat, grim monotone.

'I wouldn't worry about the young women,' said Dobie with a touch of sympathetic insight. 'It's cold logic – he'll keep 'em. Could be useful, having them available as hostages.'

'And you, sir?'

Commander Dobie took a more cautious sip of the brandy. 'Petty Officer Bell started the ball rolling – when he got back to Ayr, he didn't like what he found and tried the harbourmaster's office. What Duart told him there, plus the fact that the *Karmona* sailed, resulted in him telephoning me direct – not proper channels, but to hell with that. I came through immediately, by which time *Snapper* had discovered she was in difficulties.'

'A wire round the starboard screw.' Carrick nodded, and lit the cigarette handed him by Captain Shannon.

'Yes, we imagined that might be Blayett at work,' mused Dobie. 'Anyway, I – ah – borrowed a helicopter and pilot from the U.S. air base at Prestwick, took Bell aboard, and we rendezvoused with *Marlin* off Machrihanish Bay about half an hour later. Interesting experience.'

'Machrihanish Bay!' Carrick stared at him, and let the cigarette smoulder between his fingers. 'But the word was –'

'That there were no fishery cruisers to the west?' The chuckle came from Captain Shannon, perched primly on the edge of the starboard bunk. 'Glad to hear it, Mister. Commander Dobie radioed me he was on his way – and a little more besides. Anyway, we'd found some of the *Rachel C.* wreckage you were so interested in – part of a stove-in hull section which looked to me like no ordinary storm damage.' He gave an angry rumble at the recollection. 'I stopped an Ayrshire ring-net boat in the bay and had a personal word with the skipper. Now the word's been passed, in a way no bunch of dockside yobs like Blayett's crew, nor anyone not a west coast man born and bred is going to understand. There's a truce in force, Mister. The fishing grapevine is saying that *Marlin*'s in the south. Until this is over, no fishery cruiser will be reported anywhere near the Kintyre coast.'

'That helps, helps a lot,' agreed Carrick softly. 'But do we know where to find the *Karmona*?'

'We do, but not via Crosslodge,' cut in Dobie, tapping his glass. 'Didn't have to ask 'em, and didn't want to either. There's still no trace of Hinton, and I'm not so sure he was on his own out there. Consider your own case, for a start.'

Carrick nodded, the quiet, idling throb of the trawler's diesel loud in his ears. But the nuclear station was low on his present and personal list of priorities.

'According to the boffins, one of the most likely sources of the sediment in some of Elgin's jars is around Cara Island, to the south of Gigha.' The Chief Superintendent of Fisheries gave a whimsical shrug. 'Nowadays I spend more damned time fooling around with committees than doing an honest job of work. But for once, I'm glad – mention Gigha and nuclear power stations in the same breath to me, and I come up with just one answer. Bochan's Deep.'

Both islands a handful of miles from the Kintyre mainland, sparsely populated, and Bochan's Deep marked on every hydrographic chart as a freak hole in the sea bottom, 500 fathoms, 3000 feet of water in a single mile-wide sump!

'I know it,' said Carrick, sensing what was to come.

Commander Dobie grunted approval. 'One of those damned committees took more than a month, with me hopping in and out as Fisheries consultant, before they decided Bochan's Deep was the best place to use as a nuclear garbage dump for this part of the world. Good choice too – could have been made for the job. They call the containers coffin drums, which is a pretty good name because they're meant to stay buried.' He shrugged. 'At least, we thought they would – the ruddy things weigh over 1000 pounds each!'

'You think this Blayett trawls up these – these coffins?' queried Mamma Munsen. 'Hendrick, is this possible?'

The Norwegian scratched his head. 'Per'aps. Sometimes our own trawl brings up boulders from almost as deep. I remember one – it weighed five hundred pounds. I 'ave seen a boat bring up an aircraft engine, and another a mine. Why not these drums?'

'But this is different,' said Captain Shannon critically. 'They're looking for these drums – which must be like finding a needle in a ruddy haystack. You say Blayett has skin divers aboard, Carrick – but he couldn't use them at that depth, not unless they were top-class men with special gear.'

'Ordinary trawling might do it,' mused Dobie. 'Bochan's Deep has a flat, featureless bottom – which is why it seemed such a good choice. Fish ignore it – there's no food, no shelter, it's too deep for most weeds, there's not even the odd wreck to give 'em a home. The direct result is that fishing boats leave it alone.'

Carrick leaned forward, the picture suddenly clear. 'Take it they're dredging the drums out of the Deep, sir. Dr

Elgin's specimens came from nearer the one-hundred-foot mark, probably near Cara Island. That could be where Blayett makes the transfer of the coffin drums to this other ship, the *Bennici*.'

'Why not?' Dobie considered the possibility. 'Elgin was working off shore at Culzean, where both mild radio-activity and superheated water are being discharged. For his own pet project, he might want samples from another off-shore place where there might also be mild radio-activity, but where the water temperature would be normal. If he knew of Bochan's Deep, then Cara Island would be the nearest off-shore water to give the conditions he wanted.'

'And if the fish population was surprisingly heavy, that would explain why he was so interested – and why Joe Bruce kept so quiet,' reminded Carrick.

Hendrick Munsen, straining to keep abreast with them, gave his wife a worried glance. 'You mean the fish have this radioactivity?'

They knew what was on his mind – the kind of scare that could cause ashore.

'No, not a chance.' Commander Dobie was emphatic. 'Bochan's Deep is regularly monitored for extremely stringent safety levels. More than that, when the committee drew up the working code for dumping they based precautions on the pretty fantastic possibility that every third coffin would burst open when it hit the sea bed. They had to – some of this nuclear waste has a half life of thousands of years, which means what we dump today will still be potentially dangerous long after our great-great-grandchildren are dead, buried, and forgotten.' He dismissed the danger with a shake of his head. 'I'm more interested in how they get the ruddy things up.'

'The *Karmona*'s got first-class trawling gear, well maintained,' said Carrick soberly. 'All they'd need is a heavy-mesh trawl net, and they could lift stuff twice as heavy as these drums. As for locating, sir, what's to stop them using some form of asdic or a suspended Geiger counter?'

'Why not say underwater television?' Commander

Dobie was cynical, but didn't argue. He was thinking of other trawlers scattered around the world, Russian trawlers crammed with electronic gear which made them a superb espionage girdle. 'All right, let it pass. But what about these divers? Where do they come in?'

'Underwater transference, sir,' explained Carrick patiently. 'That way there's no direct contact between trawler and freighter. The *Karmona* brings the drums into – well, let's say about a hundred feet of water, then dumps them over. The *Bennici* comes along and collects, and the divers carry out the actual work of locating the drums on to the freighter's derrick hooks. That way, nobody is going to report they've seen a trawler and a coaster tied up and making a cargo exchange – it's an old smuggling dodge.'

'With a new use.' Captain Shannon, at any rate, was convinced. 'These two girls are the problem now.' He prowled the short length of the cabin restlessly. 'If it wasn't for them, we could go straight in, bang and bash style, and round up the lot.'

'But take a fishery cruiser within a mile of the *Karmona* and she'd scent trouble,' agreed Dobie heavily. 'Blayett is gambling, gambling that he's still in the clear, that you're still bobbing around in the ocean, either dead or the next-best thing.'

'Then *Marlin*'s got to stay in the background,' agreed Carrick. 'What we want is –' He left it unfinished, and gave Hendrick Munsen a long, searching look. 'What we want is right here, isn't it, Skipper?'

The Norwegian glanced sidelong at his wife for approval, then nodded. 'I think maybe you're damn right, Mr Carrick.' His face brightened. 'Then maybe we can fish in peace, eh?'

Carrick slept for the next three hours, a deep, thick sleep of exhaustion while *Marlin* and the *Tecta* moved northwards through the night darkness in a strange sisterhood, the fishery cruiser's radar acting as a probe for both vessels.

167

Their course was a slow wide curve, altered half a dozen times to avoid boat contacts which had appeared on *Marlin*'s radar screen. It brought them up beyond Gigha and Cara before dropping down again, still well to the west of the islands, working back towards Bochan's Deep. It was Captain Shannon's idea – the minor detail of a vessel approaching from the north, as distinct from the Firth of Clyde to the south, might be a delicate factor which would hold the balance for a few extra, precious seconds.

Clapper Bell shook him awake at 2130 hours, just as the two vessels parted company. *Marlin* was dropping back, the *Tecta* forging on alone, at a steady, unspectacular eight knots.

'Everything ready, sir,' he reported. '*Marlin*'s picked up a radar contact, an' the pack-boat's stowed aft.'

'Good.' Carrick yawned, blinked in the cabin's light, and rubbed the last traces of sleep from his eyelids. 'What's the weather like?'

'Just the way we want it,' Bell grinned. 'Easy runnin' sea, wind from the north, plenty o' cloud.' He laid a small canvas-wrapped parcel on the bunk. 'Commander Dobie gave me this for you.'

Carrick undid the package's cord lashing and nodded grimly at the contents – two heavy, regulation-issue .455 Webley automatics, each with its green webbing holster and belt.

'One of these is yours, Clapper.'

'Aye, I thought it might be.' Petty Officer Bell hefted one of the pistols experimentally, the oiled blue steel of the barrel glinting in the light. He grimaced. 'Well, for these two lassies' sake, I'm hopin' I won't need to use the business end.'

'You've checked the pack-boat's engine?'

Bell put finger and thumb together. 'Runnin' like a gem.'

Carrick swung himself from the bunk, one more item removed from his list. The collapsible pack-boat was basically two puncture-proof rubber air cylinders with a heavy rubber floor between. It had a heavily silenced jet-thrust outboard engine which could produce 40-brake horse-power and the equivalent of a land speed 50 m.p.h. It had no keel, it was a terror unless the sea was behaving – but it represented their main tool towards success.

They prepared swiftly and methodically, Carrick silent and thoughtful, Clapper Bell whistling tunelessly. Dark plimsolls, a navy-blue, throat-length sweater each, on top of dark slacks, their hands and faces smeared with black-ening which was a mixture of soot and lard from the *Tecta*'s galley – in appearance at any rate they were ready for anything.

'Your hair too,' said Carrick gently.

'Och.' Clapper Bell sniffed the greasy mixture, wrinkled his nose, but obediently smeared his spiky fair hair until it had all the appearance of an unkempt black rug. They strapped on the Webleys, and went out on deck.

The night was as Clapper Bell had said – dark, with a clouded sky, the wind whistling softly through the trawler's rigging, the sea fussing noisily against her hull as she plodded on. The *Tecta* was a deliberate glare of lights, from the triangle of fishing-signal lanterns on her foremast head to the blaze of work lamps over her fish-deck area.

They found the Munsens in the wheelhouse, Mamma at the helm, her husband by her side, right eye glued to an old brass telescope.

'I 'ave them now, which means they should 'ave us,' he said heavily. 'About a mile ahead an' two points to port. You want to see?'

Carrick took the telescope, focused through the power-ful lens, and the black outline of the *Karmona* was there before him. They were astern of their quarry, Blayett had regulation lights burning, and other lamps on deck – a good sign, on two counts. One that he was working, the other that he was still posing as just another busy trawler.

'About now, I think we should put down our trawl,' said Munsen anxiously. 'Time for you to go too, eh?' He nodded down towards the foc'sle, where half a dozen of *Marlin*'s crew under Jumbo Wills, the second mate, were

169

doing their best to appear occupied. 'I think I send them below. Too many men on deck would look wrong.'

'Do that,' agreed Carrick. 'But remember, if there's trouble, your crew rate as civilians – keep them out of it.'

Munsen's wife gave a sniff. 'Think I let Hendrick get his head shot off? How many you suppose are on this *Karmona*?'

'Twelve, maybe fourteen.'

'The one thing I don' like is what happens if your idea goes wrong.' She sighed, and pointed towards the shelf behind the compass binnacle. 'They are there, ready. Green flare if you get them off, red if . . .'

'If we don't,' Carrick finished it for her.

Hendrick Munsen cleared his throat in awkward fashion. 'Best we get ready now.'

They went aft with him to where the little pack-boat was waiting. Three of the *Tecta*'s deck hands, big, silent men who made almost a ritual of the task, helped them slide the boat into the water. She nuzzled and bounced alongside the moving trawler, still held to her by a single rope, and Clapper Bell lowered himself over, then landed in her in a sprawling crouch. Carrick prepared to follow as he heard the pack-boat's engine fire to life, then felt Munsen's hand on his shoulder.

'I would not like to fire that red flare,' said the trawler skipper quietly. 'You remember, eh?'

'I'll remember.' Carrick gave him a quick, understanding grin, and jumped down. He settled in the pitching little craft, lying flat beside Clapper Bell, and one of the trawler's crew cast off their rope. The pack-boat drifted back, swirled round and heaved as it met the trawler's wash, then broke loose from its pull as Clapper Bell eased open the throttle, heading out of the *Tecta*'s pool of light, keeping her between them and the distant *Karmona*. When they were about two hundred yards off, they saw the *Tecta* swing to port, and heard the rumble of her winch and the rattle of pulley blocks as her trawl began running out.

'That's it.' Carrick gave his companion a brief nod. 'Let's get going!'

170

Running at half-speed, the sound of her exhaust a mere chuckle of noise cloaked by the wind-plucked waves, the pack-boat began travelling . . . bumping, heaving, her rubberized floor soon uncomfortably deep in water, but the two big air cylinders which formed her hull making her impervious to the swamping she was taking.

Behind them, the *Tecta* was now down to her fishing speed, heading steadily and deliberately towards her quarry. The pack-boat's course was separate, wide of both trawlers and to port, and Carrick peered ahead, gauging their distance, calculating what was to come.

At last, he rolled over and gripped Clapper Bell by the shoulder. The bo'sun nodded, and the pack-boat's engine slowed to a whispering crawl.

'They'll be watching the *Tecta* now – but keep us about two hundred yards off their port side, Clapper. Then we wait.'

A blackened face came towards him, and Bell's teeth gleamed white in an answering grin. They came around, their boat's bow rising to each wave, her engine giving little more than steering thrust. For the moment, they were spectators, near enough to see the individual figures at work on the *Karmona*'s deck, even to pick out the silhouette of the helmsman in her wheelhouse.

The *Karmona*'s trawl was down, her hatches open, her winch engine growling as it pulled in the long wire warps. But a new decision seemed to be reached, a shout echoed across the water, the winch stopped, and the trawler slowed. Up for'ard, a cluster of deck hands began replacing the hatch covers. The *Tecta*, still a blaze of lights, was now only about a quarter of a mile away, and bearing down at the same steady speed.

Carrick took a grim satisfaction at Blayett's dilemma. He was, in theory, a perfectly innocent trawler skipper, fishing where he'd a legal right – just as much as the approaching vessel. By now, he'd have identified her – and the *Tecta*'s unhappy reputation with the Fishery Protection Service was well enough known. But the *Tecta* was too close now by any fishing standards.

171

A light began winking from the *Karmona*'s wheelhouse, a slow, angry Morse. 'K-E-E-P O-F-F.'

From the *Tecta*, an answer blinked fast and cheerful. 'T-R-A-W-L D-O-W-N B-U-T O-K.' Munsen was playing his role to perfection – with a message calculated to cause consternation aboard Blayett's craft.

'Soon now.' Carrick drew himself up into a crouch. Even if one of the *Karmona*'s crew had time to glance in their direction, the rubber boat, a mere eighteen inches of freeboard above the waterline, would be invisible to anything short of a searchlight.

The *Tecta* drew nearer, her course obvious now – cutting astern of the *Karmona*, too close for comfort when the length of both trawlers' warps were taken into account. Blayett had only one choice, to keep going, to hope that his great, deep train of cable and net might yet be clear.

The *Karmona*'s engine exhaust thundered louder, a cloud of black oil smoke shot from her stack, and her propeller wash began to grow. At the same time, her winch sang to life again.

But it was too late. The *Tecta*, still a blaze of lights, cut across her stern at about five hundred yards' distance. Beneath the water, two sets of trawl warps met, caught, tangled. Wire ropes each two and a half inches thick, with a breaking strain of nearly twenty-five tons, jerked and heaved to the sudden strain.

On the *Karmona*, the result was a bang and a flash as the winch engine burned out, followed by a mad dip of the vessel's stern. Blayett acted quickly enough, the *Karmona*'s wash churning furiously as he switched to astern and began to ease the tension on the stretching, straining cables. The *Tecta* had also lost way and was coming drifting in.

The gap between the two trawlers was down to fifty yards and still closing when Carrick was satisfied and the pack-boat began to creep closer. The *Tecta* was now almost across the *Karmona*'s starboard bow, and shouts and countercharges were blazing between the two crews – with the *Karmona*'s port beam deserted for the moment.

Another signal, and Clapper Bell cut the engine, leaving the pack-boat to drift in on her own. They touched the trawler's hull, the impact making less noise than the wave crest which followed, and *Marlin*'s bo'sun reached up to take a quick turn of the mooring rope round a deck-rail stanchion.

Carrick boarded first, his feet noiseless on the iron deck, the heavy Webley cold and ready in his fist. With a soft grunt, Clapper Bell followed him aboard, and they ducked momentarily into the shadow of an inslung dinghy. Ahead, they could see one man still in the wheelhouse, his attention fixed on the quarrel raging at the bow. Blayett was up there. They heard his angry bellow, then an apologetic, answering hail from Munsen on the *Tecta*.

But Carrick's goal was aft, where one man still lounged by the trawl winch – and beside it the companionway hatch which led down to where Helen Elgin and Shona Bruce were prisoners. He qualified that grimly . . . were prisoners if they were still aboard.

'Clapper –'

Bell nodded and crept away, moving catlike despite his bulk. The clubbed butt of the Webley rose and fell, then the big petty officer grabbed his victim, dumped him down, and signalled Carrick over.

'Get him under cover.' Carrick felt the seconds racing by – seconds before some of the *Karmona*'s crew were bound to start to work freeing their trawl, work that would have to be done from the winch area before either the shackles could be cleared and warps and net abandoned, or the warps were brought slowly up for a long, time-consuming disentanglement.

They dragged the winch's tarpaulin cover over the man, and shoved the resultant bundle into the shadow of the deckhouse.

The companionway hatch was closed, but a gleam of light came from its edges. Gently, Carrick eased the hatch cover a fraction open on its well-greased runners, and looked down. The gap gave him a narrow strip of vision across the messroom below – a strip which included the closed door of the cabin, and, an almost welcome sign in its implication, the man who sat on a chair beside it, a cigarette in his mouth, a gun laid on his lap.

Palmer! Carrick's lips parted in quick revulsion at the sight of the thin, gloomy-faced thug, remembering the hungry brutality with which the man had so readily bundled him into the trawl net, the jibes and blows that had accompanied the process.

He crouched down on the deck, gripped the hatch-cover's handle with his left hand, sent it slamming back, and at the same moment flopped clear. From below came a sudden curse, the chair legs grated, and then silence.

Another shouted exchange was in progress at the bow – but it couldn't last much longer. He saw Clapper Bell's face beneath its black-camouflage smear, and knew that he, too, was expecting the worst.

'Hey, what's going on?' Palmer's voice reached them hoarse and echoing. 'Shut that blasted hatch!'

Carrick stayed where he was, muscles tensed, gambling on a razor's edge of time. The green flare or the red – and *Marlin* committed to staying clear until one or other burst its signal.

Another muffled curse came from the messroom, then slow, cautious feet commenced ascending the companion-way ladder. He counted the rungs from one to five, now six, Palmer's head due to appear –

It did. And the trawlerman's eyes widened with fright as the Webley's barrel stabbed forward, the muzzle a scant inch from his forehead.

'I'm back,' said Carrick with a harsh, deadly emphasis. 'The gun, Palmer – easy now, finger and thumb on the butt.'

Dry-lipped, Palmer obeyed and passed up a short-barrelled .38 Colt. Carrick shoved it into the pocket of his slacks, and gestured the man back down. He followed close behind, the Webley a constant threat, and heard the hatch slam shut again above him. Clapper Bell was making his own stand on the problem of buying time.

'The key – hurry it, Palmer.'

174

'Haven't got it.' The man was sweating, his eyes told their own story of fear and indecision.

With his free hand, Carrick whirled him round, pushed his face against the nearest bulkhead, and jammed the Webley into his back. 'Hands clasped on your head.'

Palmer didn't keep him waiting.

He found the key in the left-hand pocket of the man's duffel jacket, backed up to the cabin door, unlocked it, and turned the handle.

'Time to go, girls.'

From the darkness within there came a gasp, a sudden scuffle of feet, and then they were with him.

'Webb!' Helen Elgin stared at his blackened face in momentary disbelief. 'They – they said you'd been killed!'

'I'm issuing a denial.' Carrick glanced at their faces, and saw fresh hope springing to life. 'Come on –'

'What about him?' Shona Bruce gestured towards Palmer.

'Just head for the ladder – Clapper Bell's up there.'

Helen Elgin nodded and started off. Then she stopped in startled indecision as a shout rang out above their heads. There was another cry, a shot, and a reply in the flat, unmistakable bark of a .455 Webley.

Carrick swung round, forgetting Palmer for a critical instant. He was already turning back again when he felt as much as saw a ripple of movement behind him, and heard Shona Bruce's cry of frightened warning.

Next second her slim young body slammed against his own, knocking him aside. Then she gave a second cry, this time in a high note of pain. He saw the knife clutched blade uppermost in Palmer's hand, the blood already welling from the wound that raked down the girl's left arm, and Palmer's teeth gritting in a taut-lipped grimace as he swung his arm back for another stroke. Instinctive reflex took over, the automatic in his hand slammed twice, and Palmer twitched convulsively. His back arched like a strung yew bow, and he fell.

Up above, frenzied chaos appeared to have broken

loose. Gunfire mixed with shouted warnings, the *Karmona*'s engine began increasing revolutions, and her whole hull vibrated to a dull, heavy blow.

Carrick dropped to one knee beside Palmer, and the man stared up at him. Both bullets had hit him in the chest, and he was dying.

'I should – should have finished you –' Palmer coughed, and moaned a curse, '– should have finished you that night – back at Hinton's.' The man tried to drag himself upright, but it was a last effort, and ended in collapse.

'Never mind the hatch now.' Carrick rose, put a quick, supporting arm round Shona Bruce. 'The other way, Helen – through the engineroom!'

White-faced, she nodded, followed him quickly across the messroom, stepped forward, and eased open the door. Carrick took one glance through, helped Shona Bruce across the high sill of the door, waited a fraction of a second while the other girl followed, then joined them and quietly closed the door behind him.

The engineroom, a jungle of asbestos-lagged pipes and gleaming copper tubes, was full of the heat and noise of its own being. Down by the control panel, the *Karmona*'s engineer and a greaser were at work, absorbed in their own immediate tasks. A metal-strip catwalk led across from the door to the control panel, and from the panel platform an angled ladder led up to the deck above.

'Here.' Carrick pulled the .38 from his pocket, handed it to Helen Elgin, and thumbed expressively to the door behind them. She nodded, and he eased Shona Bruce's weight from his shoulder. 'Shona – manage for a moment?'

She swayed, gripped the catwalk rail, then, as Helen Elgin's free arm went round her waist she gave a slow, determined nod.

Carrick was halfway across the catwalk before he was spotted. The greaser gave a startled yelp, grabbed for a heavy wrench lying inches from his hand – then saw the Webley, and froze where he stood. The *Karmona*'s engineer was equally intimidated, his hands rising slowly above his head.

'Turn around.'

This time, he took no chances. As each man turned, he was rapped – swiftly and scientifically on the skull. They fell side by side on the platform, removed from the reckoning until they came round.

The episode had taken less than a minute, and he spent a few more seconds throwing the trawler's throttle to the off position. Back along the catwalk, he relieved Helen Elgin of her charge and guided them both to the platform and its ladder.

Carrick went up first, the dark-haired girl leaning heavily against him, the blood flowing from her slashed arm soaking warm and stickily through the wool of his jersey, only a faint, half-stifled moan telling of her pain. Helen Elgin followed close behind, doing her best to share the burden. At the top, he stopped, turned, and put two rounds from the Webley into the gleaming metal shield of the trawler's generator housing.

There was a near-blinding flash, the dynamo grated to a halt, and the engineroom lights went out. A billow of acrid smoke reached their nostrils – and the trawler had become a lifeless iron hull, only the sigh of leaking steam and the cries and noise of the clash above remaining.

Feeling his way, Carrick levered open the engineroom hatch, eased himself up another rung, and saw the *Karmona*'s deck a shadowed silhouette, filled with struggling figures outlined in the glare of light coming from the *Tecta*.

A track of sparks soared skywards from the Norwegian's wheelhouse and burst their message in the sky – a red flare, a frantic summons to *Marlin*.

He swore softly, dragged Shona Bruce out with him to the open deck, and was helping Helen Elgin through when a huge, hairy-faced figure loped towards them, wielding an iron bar.

'Ah!' The attacker stopped the swing of the bar, blinked, and gave a quick, fantastic bow. '*Tecta*!' The Norwegian dived away again, towards a new clash in progress nearer

177

the stern. Seconds later, another man, panting and dishevelled, scurried past them in the same direction.

'Over here.' Carrick pulled the two girls away from the hatchway and in behind the shelter of the wheelhouse. Then he glanced around again. The violent blow on the hull was self-explanatory – the *Tecta* had come hard alongside the *Karmona*'s starboard bow, and the two hulls rubbed together for a third of their length. Most of the Norwegian's crew seemed to have joined the Fishery boarding party in the hand-to-hand clashes that were still raging aft.

Out to sea, a rocket burst white in the sky, then another – *Marlin* was on her way. But there had already been casualties. One man was slumped half over the *Karmona*'s bow. A Norwegian trawler hand crawled painfully on the deck nearby, and a third figure lay as if asleep on the covers of the *Karmona*'s fish hold.

Cloth ripped beside him, and Shona Bruce gave another short gasp of pain. He crouched down, to find Helen Elgin wrapping a strip of torn, lace-edged slip around her friend's arm, the blood already staining through her attempt to staunch the wound.

She looked up. 'Webb, can't we get her out of this – now? It's deep, right to the bone.'

He shook his head. Moving anywhere was still dangerous at that moment, though the tumult from aft was dying down, the signs were that the *Karmona*'s crew had had enough. 'Not yet – but in just a little while . . .' The rest of the explanation died on his lips as he spotted a movement over at the engineroom hatchway. He silenced the two girls with a wave of his hand, and waited.

The man at the hatchway took no chances. He looked carefully around while they froze silent in the shadows. Then, swiftly, he came up on deck – and Carrick recognized both man and his objective at the same moment.

Peter Blayett had escaped through the engineroom from the messroom companionway, just as they had before. Now, he was heading for the trawler's port side, to the pack-boat still tied there. He must have spotted it in the first frantic moments of alarm which had followed Clapper Bell being forced into action.

Carrick let the trawler skipper reach the deck rail, saw the tall, lithe outline tense for the jump, and hurled himself from cover, his stocky frame a battering ram which knocked Blayett sprawling from his objective. They crashed together to the deck, the Webley wrenched from Carrick's grip as its muzzle smashed against the rail's stanchion.

Blayett was armed. But, before he could swing his gun arm round, Carrick had rolled on top of him, his right hand gripping the man's wrist, slamming it back against the edge of the deck coaming, repeating the dose before his opponent could recover, hearing the man's knuckles sound like a mallet on the iron below. The paralysing force of the twin impacts loosened the trawler skipper's grip, and the automatic fell free, clattered on the metal, and fell to the water below.

A vicious knee jab found Carrick's stomach, and Blayett followed with a wildly swung left fist. The main blow missed, but his forearm jarred against Carrick's mouth, sending his head jerking back. Carrick rolled clear, then catapulted back in again, Peter Blayett's face suddenly inches from his own – and for the first time, the trawler skipper recognized his adversary.

'You!' It came as a gasping snarl. 'Should have known you wouldn't drown!'

The shock sparked a new, desperate energy from the man. He butted with his head, connected with Carrick's left cheekbone, jerked loose, scrambled to his feet, and staggered back a step as Carrick gathered himself to spring.

Somebody was running towards them from the stern, where all was suddenly quiet. Carrick was coming steadily on, like some black-faced, blood-smeared demon. Blayett glanced wildly towards the deck rail, then turned and ran clumsily towards the bow.

Carrick caught up with him just beyond the starboard side of the wheelhouse, and they crashed down again, rolling and straining, Blayett's thumbs searching for an eye

179

gouge one moment, Carrick beating him off with a single-finger throat stab the next.

A shrill cry of warning rang out behind them as they rolled again. At the same instant they were suddenly falling, falling over the open freeboard of the for'ard deck, down into the narrow, heaving gap between the two vessels.

The impact with the icy water didn't quench the struggle – it was no longer a man Carrick was fighting, but a desperate animal, insensate, temporarily beyond thought or reason. They went down beneath the surface, bobbed up, and Blayett, spluttering, changed his grip to Carrick's throat, ignoring the blows slamming against him. They sank down again, broke surface once more, and Carrick, lungs sucking for air, heard fresh shouts from above, urgent in their appeal. A rope snaked down, then another, and stark realization hit him. The two trawlers were drifting closer, the gap steadily closing.

He let himself fall back, and mustered every last remnant of strength into a sudden push forward, legs braced against the steel hull behind him. Blayett's head struck the *Tecta*'s side with a thudding force, the grip on his throat loosened, and Carrick gulped air, seeing the two steel, vice-like sides above their heads, the narrowing line of night sky, the rubbing fenders being thrown out from both boats – death in grinding, crushing agony was scant seconds away.

'Blayett – dive, man!'

The trawler skipper's face showed a sudden, horrified return to sanity. He screamed, and thrashed the water vainly towards one of the dangling ropes. Carrick jack-knifed downwards, seeking depth in the dark water, depth and more depth down between the harsh, narrowing alleyway formed by the trawlers' hulls. His shoulder grazed a barnacled keel, he turned, hands searching, gripping, pulling him round – at last, slowly releasing the last of the air in his lungs in a thankful benediction, he rose to the surface on the far side of the *Tecta*.

The first face he saw once he'd been hauled aboard was

Clapper Bell's – *Marlin*'s indestructible bo'sun had a great, welcoming beam of relief on his blackened face, a deep graze on his forehead, and one leg of his slacks was torn from ankle to knee.

'Hell, I thought I was goin' to have to explain to the Old Man about you, First Mate,' said Bell with a rare warmth.

Carrick leaned for a moment on the excited Norwegian who had pulled him from the water. 'Blayett?'

Bell's expression changed. 'It's no' a good way for any man to die. Not like that.' He shrugged. 'Well, it's over – and they're bringin' the lassies aboard now –' Then he looked out, beyond Carrick, and his grin returned. 'Here comes Captain Shannon. Och well, better late than never!'

Carrick looked round, saw the fishery cruiser pounding towards them, her high-foaming bow wave gleaming on the night sea, her searchlight swinging to pin the trawlers in its beam, and nodded. 'What happened to you?'

Clapper Bell stuck his hands in his pockets and gave a lopsided grin. 'It was nasty for a bit – a couple o' them came back to the winch, an' spotted me, then the whole ruddy ship boiled over. Still, they were so busy worryin' about me that they were caught nappin' at first when our lads came swarmin' over. Even then it was lookin' real dicey until these flippin' Norwegians joined in. Mad baskets, every one o' them –' He shook his head in unreserved admiration.

The fishery cruiser's arrival was almost an anticlimax. She came alongside the *Tecta* and within moments her crew were swarming across the two trawlers to help evacuate both prisoners and wounded from the lifeless *Karmona*. Water still dripping from his clothes, a borrowed blanket wrapped across his shoulders, Carrick talked briefly with Commander Dobie and Captain Shannon, then once again boarded the *Karmona*.

Jumbo Wills met him on the foredeck. *Marlin*'s second mate, a rough bandage round one hand, lit cigarettes for them both, then lounged back against the wheelhouse.

181

'Rough while it lasted, Webb. One of our lads killed, one of the Norwegians pretty badly shot up, both in the first rush. Another couple are wounded, and a sprinkling of cuts and bruises all round. How's the girl?'

'Needs surgical treatment, and soon. But she should be all right.' He hadn't seen either girl since they boarded the *Tecta*. Mamma Munsen had them in her cabin and was barring all visitors. 'Commander Dobie is radioing for a helicopter. What about Blayett's men?'

'They took a pasting,' said Jumbo Wills bluntly. 'Three dead – not counting Blayett. The rest – well, the lads ran a bit wild on them.' He cocked his head to one side. 'The one down in the messroom was yours, wasn't he?'

Carrick nodded. 'Palmer.'

'Well, that's one less for hanging.' Wills looked over Carrick's shoulder and stiffened. 'Hello, sir.'

Commander Dobie nodded. 'Hello, Wills. Nice job of work – now I'd like to get these hatch covers off and see just what they'd collected.'

'Aye, aye, sir. ' Wills went away, and within minutes a trio of *Marlin*'s seamen had the fish hold opened and a spotlight rigged on a cable lead from *Tecta*.

Two neat rows of white concrete cylinders lay within, sixteen coffin drums in all, each with a black on yellow radiation warning symbol, like a stylized three-bladed pro-peller, painted large along their lengths.

Dobie shook his head. 'Trouble and blood, that's what they stand for, Carrick. Well, we've pretty well cleaned up now, thank the Lord.'

'There's still the freighter, sir,' reminded Carrick.

'The *Bennici*?' Dobie sniffed. 'It'll be under escort before morning. The Navy have been wanting *Blackfish* to get into the act – well, I put her on that job. But these –' He nodded towards the coffin drums. 'What the devil do we do with them?'

'Dump them back over?' queried Captain Shannon. 'Perhaps.'

A polite cough at their elbow announced Hendrick Munsen's presence. 'You worry about these drums?'

Dobie nodded. 'I do, Skipper. And thanks for your help – though that damned red flare had us worried.'

'At the time, it seemed necessary.' Munsen had a strange expression on his face. 'Eh – maybe you should get your men off now, Commander.'

Dobie blinked. 'Why?'

Munsen shrugged. 'Because this trawler will not long be afloat.'

Carrick, like the others, stared at him. Then they saw the truth. Already, the *Karmona* was showing a faint list. At the *Tecta*'s stern, her deck hands were already slipping the shackles that held her trawl warps.

'The sea cocks are open,' said Munsen softly. 'Five minutes, gentlemen, no more.'

'Did you –' Dobie swallowed hard. 'Do you mean that –'

Munsen looked at him steadily. 'I make no answer, Commander. But is it not better that these – these obscenities go back where they belong?'

The *Karmona* sank at 2245 hours, her last trace a sighing gout of air bubbles before the iron hull and its cargo slid down to the waiting depth below. At 2305, a naval search and rescue helicopter homed on the artificial cloudlight provided by *Marlin*'s searchlight, hovered delicately above the fishery cruiser, and took on two of the *Karmona*'s wounded, one of the Norwegians who had a bullet in his chest, and, finally, Shona Bruce.

'Webb . . .' She gestured him nearer as two of *Marlin*'s seamen came to lift her strapped-up stretcher for transfer to the noisy, air-chopping machine.

'Feeling easier now?' He bent over the stretcher, Helen Elgin at his side.

She nodded. 'Webb, is it over now?'

'Nearly.'

She gave a sigh. 'Good.' Then she glanced at Helen Elgin and gave a brief wink. 'This is my share –' Her right arm twined round Carrick's neck and she kissed him firmly.

A minute later, the helicopter churned skywards and

Carrick headed for *Marlin*'s radio room. He had a long message to send, a message Chief Inspector Deacon back at Ayr was going to find both interesting and unexpected.

Ayr County's C.I.D. force spent a busy few hours next morning, climaxing shortly after nine a.m. when a tired, unshaven Chief Inspector Deacon played host to a gathering in his office.

Carrick was to one side of his desk, and in the chairs opposite sat John Stark and David Dunn. The two Crosslodge men had been collected from their homes by police car as they prepared to leave for the nuclear station, and neither seemed particularly happy about it.

'I appreciate the circumstances,' said Stark primly, sitting forward on the edge of his chair. 'But couldn't this have waited until a little later, Chief Inspector? There's the morning's mail, schedules to maintain, not to mention the Authority representatives who're waiting –'

'They know I've asked you both here,' soothed Deacon, his elbows on the desk, arrns folded. 'This won't take long, and you'll find it – interesting.'

'You've news of Hinton?' queried Dunn.

'Worried about him being still on the loose, Mr Dunn?' Deacon's expression gave no hint of what lay ahead.

The Crosslodge engineer shifted awkwardly in his chair. 'Well, after all –'

'Aye. Quite so.' Deacon nodded brusquely. 'Well, we've got some news, but in a different sort of a way. Chief Officer Carrick is the expert on what happened.' He let them turn for a moment towards Carrick, back in uniform, his face bruised, his carefully relaxed posture hiding a multiplicity of minor aches and pains.

'What's happened?' Stark blinked annoyance behind his spectacles. 'If there's news –'

'Aye, there's news all right,' said Deacon happily. 'We know how these uranium cartridges were being slipped out of Crosslodge – inside solid-waste containers. Then

184

they were being dredged up again once they'd been dumped out at sea by the Authority ship.'

'Inside the waste containers?' Dunn's voice was hoarse. 'But –'

'No "buts" about it,' said Deacon. 'Fishery Protection nailed the trawler that was lifting them back up . . . and the freighter that took them on the next stage. They went to – well, let's just say a country out in the East that's getting a bit too big for its boots.'

'Then you've got all your evidence, everything tidied up . . . except for Hinton, of course!' Stark rubbed his hands. 'First-class work – first-class!'

'It would be,' said Carrick grimly. 'But there's a snag. There were casualties out there. The men who are left could only tell us some things; for instance, how they located the coffin drums so easily. A very simple adaptation of the hydrophone system. We've already got the same equipment for skin divers, a submarine radio-telephone device. Each coffin drum had a constant signal-transmitting tube installed in the outer casing – inside, it would have been blanked off by radiation. The signal was picked up by something very like an asdic receiver aboard the *Karmona*. The rest was simple for them.'

'Simple!' David Dunn scrubbed his chin with one hand. 'But man, how did the signal tubes get into those drums, let alone the uranium cartridges?'

Carrick shook his head. 'They couldn't tell us that. The trawler skipper, a man called Blayett – he knew. So did two others. But they're dead, Mr Dunn.' He slowly and deliberately lit a cigarette. 'And Alex Hinton can't tell us either. Chief Inspector Deacon's men found his body two hours ago – found it buried under some bushes in the back garden of his cottage.'

'Hinton – dead!' Stark's face whitened at the news.

'Shot twice through the heart with a .38 Colt automatic,' said Carrick bleakly. 'Probably the same .38 that was used when I ran into trouble at the cottage. We'll soon know. Police ballistics are checking the bullets now – along with a gun I brought from the *Karmona*.'

Deacon's telephone rang. The policeman answered it with a grunt, listened, then replaced the instrument and gave Carrick a faint nod.

'But all these things – there must be an answer,' protested Dunn. 'If Hinton was involved in all this, why kill him?'

'There's an answer,' agreed Deacon, sitting back, his voice still the same soft purr. 'You want to tell them, Carrick?'

'I could.' Carrick stubbed the cigarette on the desk ashtray, then shook his head. 'I'd rather hear the story firsthand.' He leaned forward, a hard anger sweeping his face. 'Why don't you tell it, Stark?'

'Me?' The Crosslodge production director's mouth fell open. 'What do you mean?'

'That you're the inside man at Crosslodge, always were,' said Carrick wearily. 'That's how you knew Dr Elgin would be alone in his boat and passed the word to Blayett. The men who were bringing Dunn here this morning questioned him on just that point – though he didn't realize the significance. Dunn told you Helen Elgin would be at his meeting, that it meant her father would be on his own. It was just a casual aside – and it was just the opportunity you'd been needing.'

'Absolute, total nonsense –' Stark began to rise from his chair.

'If you get up or open your mouth before I'm finished, I'll knock you straight over that chair.' Carrick said it wearily, and took a deep breath. 'I've seen men die because of you, Stark. Worse, I don't know yet if enough of your plutonium uranium got through to serve its purpose. But if there is, you've helped create a threat to thousands, tens of thousands of poor, damned, everyday men, women and children who just want to live, be happy, and have enough to eat. Sit down.' He snapped the warning again. 'Sit down, damn you.'

Stark obeyed, tight-lipped.

Carrick pursed his lips. 'We wondered how Hinton got this mystery "message" that sent him rushing from Crosslodge to see Shona Bruce's father. But it came from you –

186

the one man who could give Hinton an order, swear him to secrecy, and tell him to return to his cottage immediately he'd done what you asked. Back to meet a thug called Palmer, who was waiting with a gun and a spade. Hinton knew nothing – but you wanted a handy suspect, and Palmer faked things to look as if Hinton had made a bolt. The fact that his timing wasn't quite right and I arrived a little too soon made it all the more convincing.

'But what really settled it, Stark, was a talk I had this morning. A talk with Dr Morden, at your Health Unit. Yesterday I telephoned him and asked about the ship that dumped the solid waste. He said he'd try and find out more, he knew where I was – and in all innocence he came to you. You said you'd have to look up the details, and he left it at that.'

'I told him –'

'Told him in the afternoon, Stark. Hours later – when you knew that Blayett had acted on the message you sent, and that I should be well out of everybody's way.' Carrick shook his head. 'We still don't know the number you telephoned, or who took the message to Blayett. But we'll find out.'

'At least we know how you got word from the trawler when she was at sea,' interrupted Chief Inspector Deacon mildly. 'I had a couple of men give your house a shake-down a little while back. A nice radio you've got, a very nice one, Mr Stark. An all-waveband job, an eight-valve super-het, I think they said. Still tuned to the trawler waveband too – that was a bit careless.'

'Which is how you'd know the *Rachel C.* had been sunk before anyone else,' Carrick continued the thread. 'You'd hear from the man who sank it.'

'Supposition – fancy – twisted fact.' Stark was icily calm. 'You'll be saying next that I'm carrying a gun.'

'If you were, then two of my best men would be looking for another job,' snapped Deacon. 'They had plenty of opportunity to make sure.'

'You were as sure as that. You were as sure –' David Dunn's face was grey, his voice a whisper. 'Stark!' He spun clumsily from his chair, clawing for the other man's throat. It needed both Carrick and Deacon to haul him clear and pull him back across the room. Stark got up and stood motionless, his eyes darting between the window and the door.

'The door's guarded,' Deacon told him. 'Go out the window, and you've got my blessing. It's high enough to hurt, but not to kill.'

'We're nearly finished anyway,' said Carrick bleakly. 'How you did it – well, you said yourself one man with the right knowledge and the authority could order staff to move materials, could do so many other things and cover up the traces. The final stage, getting the used cartridges into the containers, you could manage alone. The signal tubes – you instructed that directly, Stark. We've got two technicians who'll swear to it, who'll swear you told them it was a new form of warning capsule for the coffin drums in case they were disturbed. There's all the rest of your fancy story about it being covered by the Official Secrets Act, a convenient way of making sure they wouldn't talk. These capsules will hang you, Stark. I know, there was a genuine warning capsule – developed at your instruction. But the ones you issued for this "experiment" were something very different.'

'Then it's finished – just like that.' Stark took a deep breath, a little man whose inbuilt hardness still hadn't failed him. 'I refuse to make a statement.'

'We'll see. There's plenty of time,' said Deacon. 'You've a wife and kids, Stark. That's what really gets me. A wife and kids – yet you booked a single air ticket out of here for tomorrow. Getting out – getting out as soon as you heard the *Karmona* had picked up its last load.' He shook his head in disgust, then pressed the buzzer on his desk. 'John Stark, you'll be taken from here to the bar of this police station, and will be charged with offences under the Official Secrets Act and complicity in the murders of –' He broke off as the door opened. 'Ach, Sergeant, take him.

And get somebody to open this damned window. I need some air.'

Helen Elgin was still waiting in the front passenger seat of the department station wagon when Carrick left the police station a little later.

'That's it,' he told her as he settled behind the wheel. 'The rest is, to quote Deacon, "strictly routine".'

She moved closer to him. 'The less I know of it, the better. Except – this theory my father started out on. Do you think . . .'

'Fishery Research will keep working on it,' said Carrick. 'That sort of thing can take years to research, then years more to confirm.'

'We haven't got years, have we?' She looked at him, the corners of her mouth holding their own message.

'Forty-eight hours,' said Carrick ruefully. 'Then I'm due back on *Marlin*.' He heard a tap on the car window, turned, then grinned and wound down the window glass.

'Hello, Skipper – everything fixed now?'

'Everything fixed,' agreed Hendrick Munsen chirpily. 'My men in hospital will be fine, I 'ave a spare trawl, and Mamma and I 'ave been to a lawyer.'

'A lawyer?' Carrick blinked.

'For this –' Munsen drew a long white envelope from his pocket. 'Maybe you deliver it personal, to Captain Shannon?'

'What's it all about?'

Munsen beamed beatifically. 'A claim – a claim for compensation, what else? One trawl net and set of warps lost, plus compensation for two days' fishing. It is justice, eh?' Then, still beaming, he looked at them again. 'Well, maybe I just post it instead.' The envelope went back in his pocket, he gave them a drooping wink and wandered away.

'Can he do it?' Helen Elgin quivered with suppressed laughter.

'Maybe.' Carrick looked at her again, at the sparkle in her eyes, at the way the sunlight coming in through the car windows picked out the highlights in her hair, and found his mind on other things. 'But as I was saying, I've got forty-eight hours.'

She leant across him, her lips brushed his, and her hand went out and turned the starter key.